RANDOM HOUSE
CHILDREN'S BOOKS
A DIVISION OF RANDOM HOUSE, INC.

TITLE: Kiss Me Kill Me
AUTHOR: Lauren Henderson
IMPRINT: Delacorte Press
PUBLICATION DATE: January 8, 2008
ISBN-13:   978-0-385-73487-5
ISBN-10:   0-385-73487-5
PRICE: $15.99 U.S./$20.99 CAN.
GLB ISBN-13:   978-0-385-90485-8
GLB ISBN-10:   0-385-90485-1
GLB PRICE: $18.99 U.S./$24.99 CAN.
PAGES: 256
AGE: 14 & up

Please send two copies of any review or mention of this book to:
Random House Children's Books Publicity Department
1745 Broadway, Mail Drop 10-1
New York, NY 10019

KISS ME
kill me

KISS ME
kill me

LAUREN HENDERSON

DELACORTE PRESS

Published by Delacorte Press
an imprint of Random House Children's Books
a division of Random House, Inc.
New York

Delacorte Press and colophon are registered trademarks of
Random House, Inc.

www.randomhouse.com/teens

Educators and librarians, for a variety of teaching tools,
visit us at www.randomhouse.com/teachers

Library of Congress Cataloging-in-Publication Data
[CIP Information tk]

The text of this book is set in 12-point Goudy.

Book design by Kenneth Holcomb

Printed in the United States of America

10 9 8 7 6 5 4 3 2 1

First Edition

For Claudia.
You made this happen. Thanks, babe.

Acknowledgments

Huge thanks to my fantastic (and jolly pretty) editor Claudia Gabel, without whom the Scarlett Wakefield series literally would not exist. Claudia, you did a kick-ass job of editing, shaping and plot-wrangling, and I'm more grateful than I can say for your dedication and don't-quit-till-we-nail-this attitude. (Even if I did have to take a lot of headache medication during the process.) Thanks also to Kenny Holcomb for designing the prettiest book jacket I've ever had in my life. Seriously. I love it.

Also, big thanks to my never-less-than-superb agent Deborah Schneider, who is tireless, super-smart and super-chic, and a great friend. I am so lucky to have you as an agent. And thank you, Cathy and Britt, who work with Deborah and are always there for me. Even when I'm whiny.

Laura and Julia Mintz, two beautiful sweet-sixteens from NYC, gave me a lot of help with vocabulary and teenage-girl mores. Thanks, you gorgeous things. Hope you like the book!

KISS ME
kill me

PART ONE: B.D.

one

BE CAREFUL WHAT YOU WISH FOR

On January 1, I made two wishes. I know it's supposed to be resolutions, but the two things I really wanted you can't exactly *make* happen, like you can with resolutions.

I wished to kiss Dan McAndrew. And I wished to have breasts, instead of two flat pancakes on my chest. God, how I hated it when girls would come by and flick their fingers on my back between my shoulder blades and laugh mockingly because there wasn't a bra fastening there, because I didn't need to wear one.

(Actually, that's three wishes, isn't it? One kiss plus two breasts equals three, the magic number.)

Cut to June, nearly six months later, when I'd pretty much given up hope that I would get either of those things, *ever*. I had resigned myself to being flat-chested and unkissed for the rest of my life.

And then everything happened at once, and my life was changed. Though not, I might add, for the better.

Be careful what you wish for.

．　．　．

"Scarlett! Round-off, two back handsprings, back tuck! And keep it tight this time!"

I stand at the edge of the floor, bracing myself. I can do this. Ricky's halfway down, at just the right place to give me a spot on the second back handspring if I need it. But if I need it, he'll shout at me afterward.

Long and strong, Scarlett, I say to myself. *Long and strong.*

I'm running. Three steps to the round-off. Land and flip, jump up, jump back . . . my hands push the spring-loaded floor and bounce me up, feet land and I'm already jumping off my toes to the second back handspring, reaching away, reaching long . . . yes! No touch in the small of my back, which would be Ricky thinking I needed that tiny bit of help to arch on the second one . . . land on my feet again and use the momentum to rebound up, high in the air. Spot the high bar across the room, which gives me that fixed point I need to focus on for the split second before I tuck and flip myself backward like a ball through the air, thrown by an invisible hand. Land straight, knees not too bent, slightly dizzy, but knowing I made it.

"Yeah!"

Across the room, Alison and Luce, my two best friends, are clapping and whooping. I beam with happiness and look at Ricky for approval.

"Better. But go a lot longer on the second back handspring" is all he says.

4

That *is* approval, believe it or not. You don't expect bouquets of flowers from Ricky, no matter how good you are.

And then he looks at my chest.

"Strap those things down, Scarlett, can't you?" he adds. "They're bouncing everywhere—they're getting in your way when you tuck up! Jesus, where did they even *come* from?"

This is embarrassing. It's embarrassing to have Ricky talking about my boobs in front of everyone.

"Get a sports bra, for God's sake!" Ricky says, waving me away.

Like every single other girl here, I used to have a massive crush on Ricky, who's built like a rugby player—wide shoulders, muscles bulging through his tracksuit—with thick blond hair, bright blue eyes, and a really nice smile, which you get to see, on average, once a year. Ricky's incredible grumpiness is the reason my crush faded. And the insults he throws at you. And the fact that he's gay. (No reason you can't have a crush on a gay guy, of course—it just feels increasingly pointless as time goes on.)

I move to the side, giving Alison a clear run across the floor. As she starts, I walk around the edge of the gymnasium, back to where Luce is standing.

"I'm wearing a sports bra already," I say. "I don't know what to do."

"Get one of those tops with a built-in thingy," Luce suggests. "You know, the shelf support."

I pull my top a little away from my body so she can see.

"I *am*," I say hopelessly.

5

"Oh."

Luce has the ideal build for gymnastics—like a wire. She's small (you shouldn't be over five feet, five inches, that would be too much of you to send spinning through the air) and has no excess fat on her entire frame. Her breasts are pretty little points under her pale blue leotard: Luce can still wear a leotard over footless tights because she's so lean. Most of us gave that up years ago for something a bit less cruel to our curves. She wears her hair in two twisted bunches on either side of her head—a style that's easier for gymnastics, because it keeps her hair out of her way, but it makes her look even more like a little girl. Creepy old men are always giving her weird stares. But Luce is the most stubborn person I've ever met; if I suggested she change her hairstyle, she'd put plastic bobbles on her bunches and walk down the street sucking on a lollipop, just to show me.

"Maybe you should go to a sports shop and ask," she suggests.

I grimace. "They weren't much help when I went to buy the bra," I say.

Luce looks helpless. "I'd love to have ones like you," she says. "But I know I never will. My mum's flat as a board. The only time she had any was when she was pregnant with me, and she said she cried for weeks when they went down again."

"Better for gymnastics," I say.

"I s'pose."

"Lucy! Scarlett! Stop gossiping! Lucy, you're up!" Ricky yells.

I watch Luce precipitate herself into a blur of motion. She flies through the air, her twisted bunches spinning as she goes; in her front handsprings, she's almost perpendicular to the floor for a brief, breathtaking moment. Arms by her ears, legs almost straight out behind her. That's why we call that moment "Supergirl."

I think about what Luce said about her mum. If I had a mum, I could ask her about the sports bra thing. Maybe she would take me to the shop and talk to the snotty assistants.

In photos of my mum, she has breasts. That's what gave me hope that I would eventually get mine, too. They appeared practically overnight. I pretty much woke up and there they were. It feels weird sleeping on my tummy now. I can feel them underneath me, like two airbags. And when I walk around, everyone stares at them. Plum pointed them out the first day I was brave enough to walk into school in a T-shirt that wasn't huge and baggy.

"Oh my God, look at Scarlett's boobs! She looks like a porn star! Scarlett sweetie, you might want to take that Wonderbra off, it's just a little *desperate* looking, don't you think?"

That garnered a chorus of laughter from her entourage, of course. It's more than their life's worth not to laugh when Plum makes a snarky comment.

"Scarlett, stop daydreaming! Same again but better! I want really clean landings from you!" Ricky shouts.

One great thing about gymnastics: it is what it is. You land your back tuck somersault or you feel Ricky grabbing the back of your T-shirt, helping you rotate, bringing you safely to ground again. You work on things and you improve. Nothing changes in gymnastics: the rules are always the same. Stay tight, keep your hollow shape, go long, don't lose your nerve.

Sometimes I wish the rest of my life was like that, with a set of clear rules that, if I follow them, will keep me safe: sometimes I'm scared of things changing. Right now, it feels as if things are happening much too fast for me. I was so desperate to get my period. I was really late getting it—sixteen! That's *so* late!—and now that I have it, I really don't like it that much. I get the munchies the week before, and that makes me put on weight, which Ricky always notices. And when he comments on it, I get much more emotional than I used to. My hips are getting wider, which isn't good for gymnastics either.

And then there's boys. A year ago I didn't think about boys at all. St. Tabby's is an all-girls school: we don't meet any boys here. And I don't seem to meet any of them the rest of the time. Of course, there are millions of boys in London. But I hang out with Luce and Alison. Neither of them have older brothers who might bring friends round, and we don't do stuff like go clubbing or to parties.

We meet up at Luce's or Alison's and watch videos, or listen to music. Mostly Alison's, because her parents did up the basement for her, with comfy old sofas, a TV and DVD, and even a fridge so we can keep our drinks cold. It's like my home away from home, Alison's basement. (Hah. That's assuming I have a home to begin with, which I honestly don't.)

Or we go to the cinema, or to cafes, places sixteen-year-olds can hang out without spending tons of money. But we have gymnastics practice three times during the week plus Saturday afternoons, and you get quite knackered after that. In the summer we like to go swimming in the Serpentine, a sort of lake in Hyde Park. They have a sunbathing area. And we get ice cream.

God, we are the most boring girls in the history of the world.

Alison's mum, who's lovely, says we'll have all the time in the world for parties when we're older and at uni. She makes us popcorn (no butter, we're all careful because of Ricky) and buys lots of low-fat frozen yogurt for us (ditto). But for the last few months, I've been getting restless. I feel as if there's more out there. A whole world to explore. And here I am, sitting on the sidelines with my two best friends, eating low-fat frozen yogurt and watching *Bring It On* or *Stick It* for the umpteenth time. I know there's more to life than doing gymnastics . . . or sitting around watching girls in Hollywood movies doing gymnastics.

Which brings me back to boys, doesn't it?

I think about them a lot. More than Alison and Luce do, I know. It used to be just giggling about the latest boy-band singer, who we fell in love with on sight and had forgotten all about six months later, by which time we'd been madly in love with three or four other pretty-faced, snarling, skinny lead singers with messy haircuts. But now I think about real boys, not ones who are safely behind glass on the TV screen.

I say "boys," but what I really mean is Dan McAndrew.

And when I think about him, I feel like I'm blushing inside.

*   *   *

We have gymnastics practice after school, so it's six-thirty by the time we spill out from the school gates, a happy, giggling threesome. Jumping, bouncing on trampolines, throwing yourself through the air—it gives you a lot of energy. Alison, Luce, and I have been training together for five years now, and that bonds you really tightly. We've seen each other through a ton of ups and downs. Floods of tears. Frustration when you keep falling on your bum. Losing at competitions. Ricky's criticisms. Feeling fat—that's me and Alison, as obviously Luce doesn't exactly have a problem in that area. (Being fat is a really, really big deal in gymnastics. If a girl puts on a few pounds, she has a weight problem. Seriously.)

Alison is bitching about her mum and dad, who've booked a family holiday for them this August that she doesn't want to go on. I'm only listening with half an ear, because it feels as though Alison hasn't talked about anything but being-trapped-in-a-villa-in-Greece-with-her-boring-cousins for the last few months. I could recite from memory every word of her complaint.

Luce must feel the same way, because she breaks into Alison's rant, saying, "Oh look, Princess Plum's holding court again."

We look across the road to the park opposite our school. There, sitting on the stone steps leading up to the fountain in the center, is Plum Saybourne, the reigning princess of our school, St. Tabitha's.

We dump our schoolbags on the bench outside the school gates. Alison's dad is due to pick us up and give us a lift back to Alison's, where we're going to hang out. For all her bitching about her family, Alison doesn't realize how lucky she is: they're really close. They take it for granted that Alison and her friends will come back to their house after school to watch TV, raid the kitchen, and listen to music. Luce is an only child, but she's got a mum and dad who dote on her and give her anything she wants.

I'm the only one who doesn't have any of that. I have to get it secondhand, tag along in my friends' lives. I wish I had something to give in return, but I don't.

Behind us is St. Tabby's, huge, made of red brick trimmed with great swirls and curls of white stucco that looks from a distance like that nasty hard icing they put on old-fashioned cakes (the kind that little kids snap off and eat to get a sugar rush). The building's very imposing. In fact, the first time I walked down the street and realized that this was my future school, I was overawed and impressed at the same time.

However, I must also note that St. Tabby's looks like exactly what it is: important and expensive. It's one of the top three private schools for girls in London, and it's the one with the poshest location. Just inside the main entrance, in the big echoing marble corridor, is a series of mahogany panels on which is etched, in gold letters, the names of all the St. Tabby's students who got into Oxford and Cambridge, the two snobbiest universities in England. Parents cough up a lot of money to send their girls to St. Tabby's because they think they'll get the best education going, and because they want them to make friends with girls from the richest, smartest, most socially connected families.

Only it's not as easy to make friends with girls like that as parents think. Take this geography, for example (a subject every single St. Tabby's girl dropped like a hot potato as soon as they could. Geography is Not Sexy). Here we are at Point A—the bench outside St. Tabby's, where we wait for Alison's dad's Volvo to pick us up. Point B, of course, is the fountain in the small but perfectly groomed park across the street. St. Tabby's is in the heart of Chelsea, one of the prettiest, most expensive, most exclusive areas in London—naturally, the park is as lovingly tended as Plum Saybourne's manicured nails.

I can walk the distance between Point A and Point B in one minute flat. Cross the road, go up the path, and I'd be there. But the distance, socially, is immeasurable. Plum and her court are everything that's cool. They're St. Tabby's smart set, the ones who originate the fashions that all the other girls copy. They may not be the prettiest, but they convince everyone else that they are, and that's what matters.

"I like Nadia's skirt," Luce comments.

"Nadia's thin at the moment," Alison says.

"A bit too thin," I contribute.

We both know we're saying this because we feel fat. And we both know that we're not fat, unless you interpret the word *fat* to mean "has a sensible layer of flesh protecting her skin from getting sliced into ribbons by her bones." But I'm still looking at Nadia, who isn't drop-dead gorgeous, and I do see how she makes the best of herself: the makeup; the hair; the sexy, trendy little outfit that emphasizes her good points and conceals the weaker ones. That's true of all the girls clustered round the fountain: they present themselves so well, like packages wrapped in bright shiny paper, tied up with inviting satin bows, sprigs of flowers carefully slipped under the ribbon.

I can't help glancing at Alison, with her messy carroty ponytail, bare shiny face, and unplucked bushy red eyebrows. She's wearing a baggy sweatshirt, faded from hundreds of washings, and equally baggy track pants, the kind with white stripes down the side that rustle when she moves. She's a total tomboy. And then there's Luce—tiny, waiflike Luce, with her bunches that make her look barely thirteen. And me? My As for me, my track pants don't rustle, but I know they're hanging off my bum; they're so old by now that the material's all stretched. My hair is pinned back behind my ears in two tight rolls so it won't get in the way when I'm jumping and somersaulting. Not exactly sophisticated.

If we were packages, we'd be wrapped in brown paper, very battered at the corners, tied up with fraying string. I don't think this contrast has ever hit me quite in the same way before.

"Look, there's that new girl," Alison says, gesturing subtly with her hand. "The German one."

"Sophia Von und Zu Unpronounceable," I say.

We all giggle.

"She's in Latin with me," Luce says. "Ms. Hall tried to say it three times before she got it right."

"She's a countess," Alison says. "And she's rich. No wonder they snapped her up."

Being rich and titled pretty much gives you a passport to Princess Plum's inner circle.

"I heard that in Europe, if you're a count, all your children are counts and countesses," I observe. "So there are tons of them."

"Is that the same for princes and princesses?" Luce asks.

"I think so."

"Nadia's something." Alison bites on one of her cuticles and I nudge her with my knee. "I mean, her family are posh."

"But they got chucked out, so maybe that doesn't count," Luce says.

"Yes, it does," Alison insists. "You still keep the title."

Nadia's family had to leave Persia ages ago, when there was a revolution. It's been called Iran for years and years, but they still call it Persia, because that's more aristocratic. They kept all their money, though. Enough to easily make Nadia part of the inner circle.

We're all staring over at the fountain now, at the group sitting on its steps. They're all as glossy as show ponies. Polished. Their legs and hair and nails shine, reflecting the early-evening light. No pretense now among the three of us that we wouldn't give anything to be sitting with them, laughing at their jokes. Being part of the group that gathers by the fountain most evenings, hanging out with the handsomest, richest boys from St. Peter's, just down the road, is the absolute ideal of every girl at St. Tabby's.

"Plum couldn't even do one front handspring," mutters Luce.

"It'd mess up her hair," I chime in.

But we keep on staring wistfully, projecting ourselves in our imagination over there, sitting on the steps, looking as shiny and sleek as they do. Well, as some of them do. Even in our imagination, none of us can compete with Plum.

"Is Nadia waving at us?" Luce says, bewildered.

We turn round to see if Nadia's actually signaling to a girl behind us. But there's no one there.

"It does sort of look as if she's waving at us," says Alison, doing her best to sound bland and cool. But I know Alison so well that I can tell how excited she truly is. Her voice is actually wobbling with eagerness.

"Nah," Luce says dismissively. "She can't be."

Even Luce, the most unflappable one of our threesome, the most poised and quiet and self-composed of all of us, is getting, well, flapped by this. She's shifting from side to side restlessly, as if she's about to take off and start running across the street to the Promised Land where the Golden People sit and laugh as if they didn't have a care in the world.

Nadia is definitely waving. And there's no one else around but us: all the after-school activities have finished by now. The caretaker is coming over to lock up the gates. And somehow I don't think she's signaling at him.

"What should we *do?*" Alison says, her voice pitching higher with the strain. "Should we go over there?"

"No!" I say at once. "Think how awful it would be if it was a mistake!"

The picture of us doing the Walk of Shame back from the Promised Land, rejected, mocked, with Plum's laughter ringing bell-like in our ears, is so horribly vivid in all of our minds that we gulp in unison.

"Oh look!" Alison's practically squealing now. "She's standing up!"

Nadia is indeed on her feet. She smoothes down her short skirt, shakes back her lush mane of blue-black hair (what I wouldn't give to be Persian), and adjusts her designer sunglasses, pushing them slightly back on her head.

Her heels have got to be three inches high, and she wavers slightly on them for a moment before she catches her balance. Then she starts to pick her way down the stairs. She was sitting almost at the top—a sign of high favor. Plum gets to sit on the edge of the fountain, but then, Plum is the princess, and that's her throne.

Plum leans forward and says something to Nadia, something emphatic, by the way she's waving her hands around. Nadia nods, equally emphatically. She's at the bottom of the steps now. . . . She's on the path. . . . She's walking straight toward us. . . .

"Oh my God, what do you think she wants?" Alison is definitely squealing. There's no other way to describe it.

"Shut *up*, Alison!" Luce hisses. "Be cool!"

"Yeah," I say cynically. "They're probably just going to take the piss out of us. Nadia will say something nasty, we'll react, and then they'll all burst out laughing."

That's such a strong possibility that even Alison gets a grip on herself and calms down. We take deep breaths, trying to brace ourselves against the inevitable piece of bitchiness that's about to be directed our way.

Being noticed by Plum and her entourage is rarely, if ever, a good thing. In fact, it usually means tears before bedtime for the poor girl who gets singled out. One nasty comment from Plum, amplified a thousand times by her hangers-on, can burn through you like acid thrown on your face. Earlier this year, Plum pretended to mistake Luce for a third-former trespassing in the sixth-form area, much to the amusement of Plum's posse. Of course, Plum's elaborate apologies were even more offensive than the original comment—salt in the wounds. I know Luce cried herself to sleep that night and many nights afterward.

Nadia's crossed the road now, her tanned legs so thin that even her upper thighs don't brush against each other as she walks. Three steps and she'll be bang in front of us.

I swallow. Even the air has gone strangely quiet. It's like the showdown in old cowboy films, where the men squint into each other's eyes for an intimidating moment before going for their guns.

"Hey," Nadia says, looking straight at me.

Nadia isn't really pretty, but she wears a ton of makeup, like an Indian girl in Bollywood films. Foundation, lots of eye shadow, black eyeliner, and pale, golden-glossy lips (it's Miss Dior gloss. I know because Nadia is always reapplying it in class). It's very intimidating, this degree of grooming and (obviously) gloss. My hair is damp from gym, and I've probably sweated off all my mascara. I must look like a bag lady by comparison.

I can't breathe. I just know some awful comment about my boobs is imminent. She's going to say that Plum asked her to ask me where I got a hammock big enough to swing them in, or something.

"Scarlett? We were just wondering . . . "—Nadia says "we" to save face, but all four of us know it's Plum who was wondering—"if you wanted to come over and hang out? We might all go for a coffee later, or something."

I can't speak. But unfortunately, Alison can.

"Well, my dad's supposed to pick us up," she blurts out. "But I could ring him and tell him not to come."

Nadia looks at Alison like she's dandruff on her shoulder. "No, not *you*. God." She rolls her eyes in incredulity that Alison could even think for a moment that she might get an invitation to the Promised Land. "*Scarlett*," she says. "I was asking Scarlett."

Luce and Alison look at me. Their expressions are identical: a near-even blend of disbelief, jealousy, and insistence that I turn Nadia down and defend the honor of our threesome. All for one and one for all is what they want. What they should have.

And instead I hear myself saying, "Well, I suppose I could, just for a bit."

"Great!" Nadia says, sounding genuinely pleased.

I don't believe any of this is happening. It can't be me who's bending to the bench to pick up my bag; who's managing to avoid making eye contact with Luce and Alison, because I know the fury and betrayal I'll see if I catch their eyes. It can't be me who's turning to Nadia, throwing a casual "See you tomorrow" over my shoulder at the girls, ignoring their deafening silence. It can't be me crossing the road, walking side by side with Nadia Farouk, Plum's number-one sidekick, heading for the fountain.

But it *is* me betraying my friends, selling them out, leaving them behind the second something more glossy and shiny beckons. Ninety-nine percent of me is fizzing with excitement when I allow myself to think that the golden doors are really opening to me, that I can at last be part of the world I've always wanted to join.

But the last one percent is saying: Someone who would do this deserves everything she gets.

No prizes for guessing which part of me was right.

Two

THE PRINCESS FANTASY

Every little girl has a princess fantasy, even if it's only a fleeting moment here and there, watching a Disney film or picking up a Princess Barbie. Even if it makes her feel awkward and wrong, because she'd really rather be climbing trees and throwing balls while wearing the kind of tomboy clothing that would make Princess Barbie faint in horror.

A girl can't grow up without having princesses rammed down her throat to some extent. They come with all the best adjectives. Beautiful. Perfect. Worshipped. A princess is the kind of girl who doesn't need to _do_ anything to get noticed, apart from walk into a room looking drop-dead gorgeous.

Alison, Luce, and I all love those films where the ugly gawky girl in glasses gets told that she's really a princess, a fairy godmother spinning in to transform her magically (i.e., without plastic surgery) into a knockout beauty in contact lenses (maybe colored ones). I think we all used to go to sleep at night cherishing that fantasy. But then harsh reality kicked in. For me it was at fourteen, when I realized that I wasn't the princess in my life story.

Someone else was.

I expect every school has a reigning superstar, the ideal to which every other girl aspires. When I first arrived at St. Tabby's, I thought that girl was Cecily, a burgeoning super-model who was about ten feet tall, weighing in at about 110 pounds, with blond hair to her waist and eyes as blue as Wedgwood china. Cecily was so beautiful she could come into school with a stinking cold, eyes red-rimmed, nose swollen, wearing jeans and a big sweater, and still look more beautiful than everyone else at St. Tabby's put together. But Cecily was too shy to say a word to anyone, which put her out of the princess stakes.

Because princesses need to rule. They need a court to command. And for that, they need to be able to give orders and keep discipline in the ranks. And there's no one better at ruling a court than Plum Saybourne.

I've reached the foot of the fountain steps. The sun is shining straight into my eyes, dazzling me. Typical of Plum to seat herself with her back to it, providing herself with a golden halo.

Nadia is behind me, and as I pause, not knowing where to sit, she says impatiently, "Go on, then!"

But I don't know which step I should be sitting on, or how high to climb. It sounds ridiculous, but I know if I get it wrong I could be in trouble.

"Scarlett!" drawls Plum, flicking back her hair. "Nice of you to join us. You know everybody, right?"

It's like she owns the park. I have to admire her blatant sense of entitlement. Must be nice to be that self-confident.

Plum gestures to a step below her. "Well, sit down."

Nadia follows behind me. She tugs on her skirt hem and sits down carefully, making sure she's got enough material in front of her to at least cover her knickers. Her skirt is so short she can't even cross her legs.

I sit down next to her. It seems a safe choice, considering it was Nadia who invited me. I feel like such a frump in the track pants I pulled on over my gym shorts. I never worry about what I look like after gymnastics, because I'm just going home to shower, or back to Alison or Luce's. Now my thighs look all bulky because of the two layers of clothes I'm wearing, particularly sitting next to Nadia, with her skinny, naturally pale-brown legs.

"So, Scarlett," Plum continues. "You've certainly developed overnight, haven't you?"

All the girls laugh sycophantically. That's how it works. Plum rules with an iron fist in an iron glove.

There doesn't seem to be much of an answer to that, so I don't say anything. Apparently, Plum isn't expecting a response, because she plows right ahead with her next comment.

"Let's all be careful not to bump into Scarlett from behind," she says. "She'll fall right on her face. What are those, Scarlett, thirty-four Ds?"

God, this is humiliating. The truth is that I'm a bit con-fused about how to measure them. I was going to ask Luce and Alison to come with me to one of those big department stores where the saleswoman does it for you, but I can't think about Luce and Alison right now, it makes me feel too guilty.

"Venetia would kill to have thirty-four Ds, wouldn't you, Venetia?" Plum says.

"Oh *God*, yes," says Venetia, quite unembarrassed.

Venetia is a super-posh girl, flat-chested, mousy-haired, freckled in all the wrong places, with a bum as wide as the Channel. But she's got the absolute confidence that comes from her family's having owned most of the North of England since Queen Elizabeth came to the throne—that's Elizabeth I, of course.

"I'd bloody love it," Venetia says wistfully. "Did you see that picture of me in *Tatler* at Ross's seventeenth birthday party? I looked like a boy in a frock! I showed it to Mummy and told her I was *dying* to have a boob job, but Mummy says I have to wait till I'm eighteen and get my trust fund. She won't pay for it herself, the cow."

"God, considering how much surgery your mum's had, that's a bit rich," Plum comments.

"I *know*," Venetia sighs. "*So* unfair."

Plum talks about plastic surgery with the airy careless-ness of someone who doesn't remotely need it—or certainly not for decades to come. As befits a princess, she's naturally gorgeous, though she certainly maintains herself well. She has long, shiny hair the color of autumn leaves (i.e., brunette with lots of expensive coppery highlights), slightly slanty green eyes (contacts, I swear), and blusher-tinged cheekbones high enough to give her a haughty expression.

"I must say, Scarlett, you look a bit pink and sweaty," Plum comments.

"I just came from gymnastics," I say defensively.

"*Much* too energetic for me," Plum sighs. "I get tired just walking on the treadmill, don't I?"

There's a general murmur of assent.

"Can someone lend Scarlett some lip gloss, or something?" Plum asks with a hint of disdain. "I mean, she's looking a bit too *fresh-faced*, don't we think?"

This is classic Plum, ending almost every sentence with a question that you're not really meant to respond to—out loud, anyway. A girl sitting below me holds up a tube of Lancôme lip gloss. Someone else hands me a slim, handbag-sized spray of Elizabeth Arden Sunflowers. Mumbling thank-yous, I duly smear my lips with gloss, and spritz myself with the perfume, which is, much to my relief, light and not at all cloying.

I hand the gloss and perfume back to their owners. Just as I'm sitting back up again, a rustle runs through the group, as if we were a pile of autumn leaves lifted by the wind. Lips are bitten, cheeks are pinched, and shoulders are straightened. Suddenly, everyone's on full alert.

Plum is flicking her hair and swinging her legs as if she's signaling with them. And in a way, she is. She dips her head a fraction to look over the top of her designer sunglasses.

The other girls are trying so hard not to turn their heads that they look frozen in place, like a whole series of statues; Plum's the only one moving.

I can't help it. I'm curious. I turn my head to look.

Oh God. I'm such an idiot. I was so swept away by the flattery of being invited to join Plum's coterie that I forgot briefly about one of the main reasons that entry to this group is so prestigious: it comes with access to the sixth form of the neighboring boys' school.

But only the most eligible boys. The richest, the poshest, the best-looking. Five or six of them are coming up to the fountain right now, slouching, their hair artfully messed up and hanging over their faces. They're doing their best to look as casual as possible, as if they couldn't care less about hanging out with this group of girls. But I can tell how keen they are to see us by the very fact that they're looking so exaggeratedly laid-back, almost as if they barely notice us sitting round the fountain till they're standing right in front of it.

I look at them all, and my heart sinks—he's not here.

"Hey, Plum," the leader says.

"Oh, hi, Ross," Plum says equally lightly, playing along with the game of fancy-seeing-you-here.

"What's up?"

"Nothing much," Plum answers. "We thought we might get a coffee later or something."

"Cool."

This must be the Ross of the seventeenth-birthday celebration that was considered socially important enough to be

26

photographed for *Tatler*, the snobbiest glossy mag for posh people in the country. I'm convinced now that Plum has invited me here to play some really cruel joke on me. I fit in with this smart set about as well as a troll would at a princess-only slumber party.

The boys arrange themselves around the fountain, most of them leaning against it. Ross pulls out a pack of cigarettes, which is a cue for all the smokers present to light up themselves. Lighters click, matches snap, little flames shoot up. Everyone takes their first drag and then breathes out in unison. I look at Ross while everyone is distracted. He's in the middle of a nasty acne outbreak, but he looks so unfazed by his bright red itchy-looking spots that he almost carries them off. Posh people really do care less about what the rest of the world thinks. Maybe I can learn the secret of that from them. That's what I want most in the world: to lose my self-consciousness and ooze this kind of confidence.

"Cigarette?" asks a boy standing next to me.

"Uh, no, thanks," I say.

"Don't smoke?"

I shake my head.

"Very sensible. Isn't any good for you, is it?"

"Well, I do gymnastics," I say. "I mean, I don't want to run out of breath halfway through a routine."

"Gotcha," he says. "You mind?"

He gestures to the step I'm sitting on. I nod a bit shyly, and he sits down next to me.

"I'm Simon," he says with a warm smile.

I smile back. "Scarlett."

Simon isn't bad-looking, but there's nothing distinctive about him either, apart maybe from his bright pink cheeks. He has fair hair, brushed forward, and he's maybe a little overweight, though it quite suits him. His mouth is very red, with puffy lips, in that way that happens sometimes with people with really fair skin and blond hair.

"I think I've seen you around St. Tabby's," he says. "Don't you hang out over there some afternoons?"

He gestures to the bench where I was waiting today with Alison and Luce. Automatically, my eyes follow his hand, and I see with a great deal of relief that Alison's dad must have come to pick her and Luce up; there's no one there.

"Yeah, sometimes I'm there with, um, friends from gymnastics."

I have a bit of trouble saying the word *friends*, out of guilt, but Simon doesn't notice.

"Right." Simon blows out a puff of smoke. "You all look so . . . healthy."

I laugh. "That's a polite way to put it. Plum just made me put on some lip gloss because I looked all sweaty."

For some reason, I get a little flush of pleasure after I mention this; I can't help but think it was nice of Plum to try to help me look pretty, even if she was probably only doing it so I would fit in better with her group. But if she didn't think I would fit in, why did she invite me over?

I ponder this, confused.

Simon clears his throat. "Hmm, well, I wouldn't think you

needed that," he says. "I mean, you're very pretty already, you don't need anything else." I feel myself blushing, and am thankful that there's a buzz of conversation now, so that probably no one heard him. I really don't hang out with boys that much; I'm not used to this kind of thing, and I don't know what to say in return. "Thank you" sounds much too prissy.

Still, Plum must have sensed that Simon just paid me a compliment. "Is Simon flirting with you, Scarlett?" she says, leaning down. "You've got to watch him, you know, he's terribly naughty."

Now it's Simon who's blushing; he's so pink already that he goes bright red.

"Still, he's a great catch!" Plum adds, winking at me, which just completes my and Simon's embarrassment. Neither of us can look at each other. I stare at my feet. Simon looks straight ahead, dragging so hard on his cigarette that it looks as if he's going to drain it down in a couple of seconds.

"Hey, everyone, what's up?"

It's a new voice, calling from further down the path. I register that its owner must be pretty confident to announce his arrival that clearly, and curiosity makes me turn to look.

I gulp so hard my throat hurts. I actually think I'm going to choke. My eyes water, and I start to cough. Simon thinks it's because of the smoke from his cigarette, and instantly stubs it out on the stone, apologizing profusely.

But I barely hear what he's saying. When I've got my breath back, I realize that my heart is pounding so hard I can't hear anything over the racket it's making.

29

This, more than anything else, is the reason I was so eager to jump at Plum's invitation. *This* is what I've been staring at longingly from that enormous distance that separates the bench outside school from the Promised Land here at the fountain. *This*, the opportunity to be so close to the hottest boy I've ever seen, close enough now to reach out and touch him, now that he's coming up the steps. I sit on my hands so I won't be tempted to do that very thing.

"Hi, Dan," says Simon.

And Dan McAndrew—gorgeous Dan McAndrew—jumps the last two steps, swings himself up onto the lip of the fountain so easily you'd never know what prime, protected real estate it is, and actually dares to put out a hand and ruffle Plum's hair.

"Having fun, Plum?" he asks cheerfully. "Si, all right, mate!"

He leans over to grab Simon's hand and do one of those funny twisting handshakes that boys seem to consider so essential. I always thought his eyes were gray, but now I realize that they're just as much green as gray, the color of a lake in winter, and so thickly fringed with dark lashes that it almost looks as if he's wearing mascara. His dark-brown hair is falling forward in a silky wash over his forehead. I long to reach up and push it back.

Dan McAndrew is six feet tall, with wide shoulders and long legs. He's on the school cricket, rugby, football, and tennis teams. He plays violin in the school orchestra, and he's on the debating team. He's as handsome as the lead singer in a boy band. He's always got a ton of friends hanging round with him.

Plum is rearranging her hair, smoothing it out with her fingers, frowning crossly at Dan for having messed it up. She shifts along the stone lip of the fountain, pointedly turning her back on him, facing Ross instead.

"God," she mutters, "he's such an *oaf* sometimes."

I'm watching her, amazed that anyone could actually *complain* about being touched by Dan McAndrew, when I hear him say "Hi," and it takes me what feels like hours to realize that he's talking to me.

I look up and meet his eyes. Then I faint. But just for a fleeting moment. I get such a quick grasp on myself that I don't think anyone but me noticed that I actually lost consciousness.

"Hi," he repeats. "I don't think we've met, have we? I'm Dan."

It's all I can do to get any words out at all. I can barely remember my own name.

"I'm Scarlett," I manage.

"Great name," he says appreciatively. "It suits you."

"Really?"

I must be goggling at him. I've always felt that Scarlett was a real curse of a name. In my eyes, you either have to be a redhead or fantastically beautiful, like Vivien Leigh in *Gone with the Wind*, to be called Scarlett.

I'm not a redhead. My hair's medium brown, not particularly interesting. And let's just say that we can rule out the fantastically beautiful part as well.

But Dan McAndrew is smiling at me, his gray-green eyes are sparkling. At least I can tell that he's not setting me up

31

for a fall, saying something nice just to see if I'll believe him, before cutting the ground out from under my feet.

Which means . . . which means . . .

Behind his shoulder I see Ross clicking at a Zippo lighter that isn't working. He shakes it angrily, and tries again. No go.

"You try, mate," he says, chucking it to Dan. "You've got the magic touch."

"Do something, Ross!" Plum adds petulantly. "I'm *dying* for a ciggie."

Dan shakes the Zippo, gives it one sharp tap on the fountain's edge, and flicks the wheel. It catches.

"Thanks," Ross says, taking it from him. "Here you go, Plum."

He bends toward her, lighting the cigarette that she dangles at the end of her fingers, making him come into her space, do all the work. I admire her technique. Ross lingers a little too long, staring at her beautiful profile, before he sits back again.

"Plum, you shouldn't smoke," Dan says, sitting up again. "And you shouldn't either, Ross. It's disgusting."

"Oh, stop nagging, Dan. You're worse than my bloody mother," Plum snaps, not even looking at him.

"Yeah, Dan, pack it in," Ross agrees.

Dan's forgotten about me for the moment; his attention has been drawn elsewhere, and I have to admit, I'm almost relieved. Having Dan McAndrew look at me, *really* look at me, his gray-green eyes focusing on mine, was so intense I had trouble breathing. I'm grateful for a respite.

"Sorry about making you cough," Simon says to me.

I don't have any problem looking at Simon, because I don't fancy him. He's pink and white, like a Battenberg cake with yellow icing on top, which is his hair. His eyelashes are so pale yellow that they practically disappear into his face. He's staring at me intently, but I can't quite remember what he's referring to.

"Oh, that's okay," I say.

He clears his throat. "Um, are you coming to the party on Saturday?"

This is way too much for me.

"I don't know anything about it," I confess. No point pretending to be cooler than I am.

"It's at Nadia's," Simon says. "Her parents are away."

"Her parents are *always* away," says Venetia, giggling. "I'm beginning to believe you don't actually *have* any parents, Nadia!"

I sneak a glance at Nadia. She's frowning and biting her lip, so cross with Venetia that she's forgotten to care about messing up her lip gloss.

Venetia's too insensitive and busy laughing at her own joke to notice that she's upset Nadia.

"When are we going to have a party at *your* house, Venetia?" Plum says with a little smile.

This must be a nasty dig, because Venetia stops laughing so suddenly it's as if Plum had flipped a switch in her back. Having dealt with Venetia, and underlined her power in the process, Plum gives Nadia a single swift glance, which seems to encompass me, and sits back on the fountain step, looking smug.

33

"Yeah, come to the party, Scarlett," Nadia says. "Everyone will be there. You're not doing anything else Saturday night, are you?"

I shake my head, though it's a lie. I was supposed to see a film with Luce and Alison. This is a whole series of betrayals, I realize, not just the one. I feel terrible. But I also feel incredibly excited that I've been invited to Nadia's party. I'm so confused I don't know what to think.

"Great," Simon says enthusiastically. "That means you're coming, right?"

I nod.

And then I look up at Dan, hoping he'll be as enthusiastic as Simon. He meets my eyes and smiles at me, and my heart turns over.

Hah. Little do I know that by the end of that longed-for party, I'll be looking back and yearning for the chance to take back that nod. To rewind this entire encounter, like running a DVD backward on fast speed, as I get up, walk backward down the path, seemingly followed by Nadia, cross the road backward (not too safe, that, but I don't get knocked over), reach my friends, and press Stop and then Play again—and change the outcome. To say to Nadia, "No, thanks, I won't come and hang out with you if Alison and Luce can't come, too."

But by the time the party ends, it'll be too late.

Dan McAndrew will be dead.

And it'll be me who killed him.

Three

JEANS GO WITH EVERYTHING

You can only worry about what's going on at the time. That's one of life's weird ironies. Because so many times afterward, you look back and think, *God*, that's *what I was fussing about?* Talk about a total lack of proportion! I'd give anything to go back in time and be dealing with those tiny little issues, instead of the great big problems I'm wrestling with now.

But hey, welcome to the wonderful world of hindsight.

Because I don't know right now that I'm being set up. I don't know that Dan McAndrew is going to die at that party. All I *do* know is that I'm obsessed with two worries going round and round in my head, and (because I can't see into the future) they seem like the two most important things in the world, like an eclipse blocking out the sun, so I can't focus on schoolwork, gymnastics, anything but them: (a) Will Luce and Alison ever forgive me? And (b) What the hell am I going to wear to Nadia's party?

I'm horribly ashamed to admit this, but the second question is the one that's bothering me more. And I know what an awful person that makes me. I should feel terrible about turning my back on my friends like that, and I do. When I think about Alison and Luce, and the fact that they're sending me to Coventry at the moment—not speaking to me, not looking at me, basically pretending I don't exist—I get an awful sinking feeling in my stomach.

And when I think about the party, I feel like sick is rising in the back of my throat. Why on earth did I agree to go? I barely know anyone to say more than two words to. I don't travel in their world in any way. Their specialist subjects are the classics. And I don't mean Latin and ancient Greek. I mean the *real* St. Tabby's classics: where to get the best manicure, which is the best month to go to Saint-Tropez, which boys will raise your social status, and how to get on the special pre-sale-viewing list for whichever shoe designer is hot this year.

And no, I'm not familiar with these topics from personal experience. But if you have any classes with Plum or Nadia or Venetia, or if you're simply stuck behind them as they take their time going upstairs in those wobbly stilettos, you can't help learning more about them than you ever wanted to know. It's all they bang on about. You'd think St. Tabby's was a Swiss finishing school with classes in flower-arranging and how to get out of Porsches, the way they carry on.

And yes, I'm jealous of how glamorous and photographable their lives are, and that's why I sound bitter. No point denying that, is there?

I stare at the contents of my wardrobe. This is a joke. I don't know why I'm even looking. I know already that I don't have anything to wear to a party at Nadia Farouk's penthouse flat in Knightsbridge. That in itself—not having anything to wear—wouldn't be an insuperable obstacle. The true problem is that I know enough about fashion to recognize that I don't have the right thing to wear, but not enough to know what that would be.

Hell and damnation.

I glance around my room, which doesn't represent me, because this isn't my home. It's a guest room, complete with white walls and tasteful engravings of fruits and flowers, which are echoed in the chintz curtains and bedspread. Sounds a bit like a classy hotel, doesn't it? I'm not allowed to put up posters, or even framed prints. No making holes in the walls. In a way, it's a little girl's dream room: it's very pretty. But it's not me. It's never been me.

No wonder I've been spending all my time hanging out with Alison and Luce. But suddenly I feel as if I've been hiding in Alison's basement for the last few years: hiding from everything. Life. Boys. The universe.

And though I know that's a gigantic exaggeration—after all, it's not like I was invited to a ton of parties I didn't go to, it's not like a ton of boys asked me out and I turned them all down—I'm also aware that there's more than a grain of truth in it. I've been at school, or doing gymnastics, or hanging out with the girls I met through gymnastics, for the last few years. I didn't take any risks—apart from throwing myself through the air trying to do a twisting back layout and land on my feet rather than my head, of course.

It's not surprising that I grabbed at the first thing resembling security that came along—drowning girl and life preserver ring spring to mind, though it's such an obvious analogy that my English teacher would write "NO NO NO LAZY LAZY!!!!!" if I tried to use it in an essay. (She's not big on sparing your feelings.) But maybe it's time to push aside the life preserver and start swimming on my own?

Not that I have much choice, actually. I doubt that Alison and Luce will ever speak to me again.

I sit down on the corner of my bed and stare out the window at the view. Thick green leaves from tall, sweeping trees frame two elegant large white houses across Holland Park, which is the wide street on which this house (equally white, equally large, equally elegant) is set. Occasionally a red double-decker bus passes by along Holland Park. I can see the top deck, but its passengers aren't remotely close enough to peer into my window. These houses are built on a slight rise, and their lawns slope down gently to high stone walls, lined with trees, to provide plenty of shade and privacy. I've spent a lot of time lying out on the lawn, reading in the sunshine. By myself, of course, because I'm not allowed to bring any friends back to the house. That's one of the conditions of living here.

It's lonely. But I do have the whole attic to myself. Which includes my own bathroom.

Looking at the view from my bedroom window is what I always do when I'm confused, or upset, or unhappy. Rain or shine, gray skies or blue, it never fails to center me and calm me down. I think: *If this were a project at school, an exam I wanted to pass, what would I do?*

And then I think: *Research. I need to research my way through it.*

For the first time since being invited to that party, I feel as if I might be able to get things just a bit under control.

*   *   *

"Oh my *God*! *Look* at that bag! It's the *definition* of pretty!" exclaims Girl A.

"Oh yah!" replies Girl B, which is how really posh girls say "yes." "If that bag was a girl, all the boys would be totally in love with her."

This exchange is followed by a round of self-conscious giggles at their own cleverness.

I shrink against the changing-room wall. And not because of their idiot banter—it's like hearing boys on the bus repeating lines from comedy films that were hilarious on-screen, but crash and burn in the mouths of talentless morons. The talentless morons fall about laughing. Everyone else roll their eyes and turn their iPods up.

I'm cringing because I know those voices. The first one is Venetia and the second one is Sophia Von und Zu, the German countess with wads of money coming out of her ears. I peek through a tiny chink in the curtains just to confirm it. Yup, there they are. Confidence is a weird power.

Horse-faced, big-bummed Venetia is standing there with as much self-assurance as if she owned the shop. And tall, slender, blond Sophia, with smooth china-white skin and enough money to buy the shop here and now, has the droopy shoulders and slumping posture of a rag doll with really low self-esteem.

"Excuse me," Venetia says, I presume to the shop assistant, "do you have this in any other colors?"

"No, I'm afraid not. Just the yellow," says the shop assistant.

"Oh, *God*, how *upsetting*!" Venetia exclaims, as fervently as if she'd been told that one of her best friends had been taken to hospital.

"*So* disappointing!" Sophia chimes in. It's obvious she thinks that agreeing with everything Venetia says will keep Venetia as her friend. And Sophia is absolutely right.

And then I nearly jump out of my skin, because the girl who's helping me pulls lightly at the curtain of my cubicle and says, "How's it going in there? You need any other sizes?"

"Uh, no," I mumble, trying to keep my voice low so Venetia and Sophia won't recognize it. "I'm fine."

"Great," she says brightly. "I'll give you some time. You've got a lot to get through in there."

I certainly do.

This boutique is like a jewel box. It has pale-blue Ultrasuede walls, shiny emerald floor, chrome-and-silver display racks, a series of minichandeliers trembling with crystal drops hanging from the ceiling, which is painted with a mural of silver clouds on an azure background. The changing room has an Ultrasuede upholstered bench and the curtains are layers of blue and green chiffon. And on the long rail, which I turn to look at now, is hanging a whole row of clothes that the very helpful salesgirl has picked out for me. Clothes in greens and burgundies and pale mauves that, she says, suit my coloring; clothes that, hopefully, cling in all the right places while draping tactfully over the others. Clothes that will make me look as if I belong in a place like this.

Because if I can look like I belong here, in this gorgeous temple to beauty and fashion, then my odds of looking like I fit in at Nadia's party are infinitely raised.

Clearly, my trendy-boutique research (I scoured *Teen Vogue*, *Elle Girl*, and a slew of other magazines looking for shops which sounded like places Plum and her crew would go) was very successful. Too successful. I hadn't bargained on running into members of Plum's set during the buying process.

I realize I'm going to have to hide out in the changing room the entire time they're here. Because if they see me, they'll know I'm here buying clothes for the party, and then I might as well not go at all, because everyone will laugh at me because I was so freaked out by the invitation that I had to run out to the most expensive boutique in super-chic Notting Hill and shop like a pathetic, desperate, socially insecure maniac, but I have to go, because Dan McAndrew is going to be there, and he said my name suited me—

Calm down, Scarlett, for God's sake! You're hyper-ventilating, you stupid cow!

I close my eyes for a moment. Over the hypno-relaxing-trippy music that's playing, I hear Venetia's voice. Actually, I could hear Venetia's voice over zombie death metal, cranked up to full blast. She's got one of those grating, high-pitched upper-class voices that could cut through steel faster than a circular saw.

"Oh my God, no, you can't wear Blue Aeroplanes! Put those back at once!"

"What do you mean?" Sophia sounds baffled, as am I.

"You can't wear Blue Aeroplanes jeans! Only Plum can wear Blue Aeroplanes!"

"Are you *serious?*" Sophia says.

"Fine. Don't believe me. Buy them and see what happens."

"What'll happen?" Now real doubt is creeping into Sophia's voice.

Venetia heaves a giant sigh. "Plum will send you to Coventry for weeks. That's what she did when Nadia bought Blue Aeroplanes. Don't you remember?"

"No, I don't! When was that?" Sophia sounds petrified.

"Last autumn. After half-term. You *must* have been there."

"I was in Kenya the week after half-term! On safari with Mummy and Daddy!" Sophia realizes. "But I do remember, I came back and we weren't allowed to talk to Nadia. Only no one told me why, and I didn't want to ask."

42

I grimace. Sophia is such a pathetic sheep.

"Well, that's why," Venetia says. "And now you know."

I hear the sound of hangers shifting as, I presume, Sophia fearfully slips the pair of Blue Aeroplanes jeans back on the rail.

"Secretly?" Venetia adds, in what she thinks is a lowered voice. "And promise you won't tell?"

"Oh yah, *absolutely!*" Sophia sounds very excited.

"Nadia looked better in the jeans than Plum did. That's why Plum got so angry. You know she doesn't have much of a bum."

"*Gosh,*" Sophia says.

"I heard Nadia cut the jeans up and sent them to Plum, and that's when Plum took the Coventry thing off and we could talk to Nadia again," Venetia continues. "But that's just a rumor."

"Oh yah, of *course,*" Sophia says.

They both sound very subdued now. I know they believe the part about Nadia cutting up the jeans.

And so do I.

"Well, there's nothing in this bloody shop today," Venetia says bluffly. "Since they only have that bag in *yellow.* God. Do you want to get a soy latte?"

"Love to!" Sophia sings out.

Honestly, I'm surprised Sophia doesn't bleat instead of talk. I bet if Venetia had asked her if she wanted to get a slice of dead rat fried in batter, she'd have agreed. Anything to fit in.

Mind you, it's hypocritical of me to complain about that, isn't it? What am I doing here if not spending a fortune on clothes that will help me fit in?

I nose slowly through the curtains to make sure they've gone, like a mole trying to see if it's safe to come out of its hole. When I've got enough of my face (about the amount you have out of the water when you're floating in the sea) through the gap in the curtains to be sure that the coast is clear (goodness, I'm full of metaphors today) I emerge.

"That looks really nice," says the shop assistant from across the room.

I turn to look at myself in the long mirror in its twisted silver frame. I already had a look in the changing room. I'm not an idiot—I know better than to walk outside without checking first to make sure I don't look like a fat sausage squeezed into a skin too small for it.

I'm wearing an aqua green top in a silky material, with lots of straps, including one that runs diagonally across one shoulder and down the back. The material is suspended from the straps in a series of gathers and angled folds that looked on the hanger like someone had taken drugs and gone crazy in the sewing room, but on me actually hang really nicely. It's a bit like drapery from a Greek statue, and somehow, miraculously, I look grown-up and graceful in it.

The salesgirl has also found me a pair of jeans that work. I.e., I didn't pull them on, stare at myself in the mirror and think *Thunder thighs, elephant legs*, and burst into tears. Not too skinny, not too baggy. Nice dark denim, which is always safe. Pale denim is only for girls so thin and confident that they can wear stuff that's so out of fashion it's just about to come raging back in again. And I am not one of those girls.

Thank God I've got a pair of jeans that fit. I know it'll be okay to wear them to the party. Jeans go with everything.

"Do the sandals fit?" asks the assistant.

"Yeah, I think so," I say.

To my embarrassment, I actually have to think about that, since I am so not used to wearing three-inch heels. I take a few steps, and I don't fall over or twist an ankle.

"Um, you might want to do your toenails if you're going to wear open-toed shoes," says the assistant nicely.

I look down at my craggy, unvarnished toenails. The contrast between them and the strappy gold sandals is so awkward it's comical. I'm like a little girl playing dress-up in her mother's shoes. Only this isn't dress-up anymore. If I'm going to wear the princess shoes, if I'm going to go to the princess party, I'm going to have to act my age. I'm sixteen. I'm not a little girl any longer.

She comes to stand behind me, tugging and adjusting the gold and brown leather belt and the drapes of the green top so it hangs just right. In the long mirror, I watch what she's doing. I take a whole series of mental notes. I want to be able to reconstruct this perfectly for Saturday night.

"Some earrings," she's muttering as she touches my hair. "Take this back off the face. You need blusher. And a lot of

45

eyeliner. A *lot*. I'll set you up with a nice little makeup kit. Oh, and do you have a pretty bra? Because that one's showing, and it's not exactly, hmm . . . "

In the mirror, I watch myself go bright red. Not exactly the kind of blush she was recommending. I shake my head wordlessly.

"No problem, I can tell you exactly where to go. Now, why don't you come over here and pick out some nice earrings? Wow, this is so much fun!"

I hope she's on commission, because she's being really nice to me. Not at all patronizing, which is what I was terrified of. Like the obedient lamb I accused Sophia of being, I walk dutifully over to the counter.

This is all going to cost me a fortune.

Lucky, really, that I have a trust fund.

SHINY HAPPY PEOPLE

The building is a sheer sheet of glass and steel and lights are gleaming behind the windows. I was careful not to show up before ten-thirty, knowing that nothing would be worse than to be the first person at the party. I think I can hear laughter coming from somewhere up above, but maybe I'm hallucinating it, out of nerves. That not-so-rare psychological condition where the sufferer thinks everyone is laughing at her.

There's a cantilevered glass roof slanting over the entrance. The doors (also glass, I'm sensing a theme here) slide apart as I step onto the gray carpeting that covers the pavement in front of them. They hiss shut behind me with a quiet thunk. The atrium inside is just as impressive as the facade of the building, illuminated by a gigantic chandelier-type-thing made out of what looks like millions of bits of glass from a shattered bus shelter.

"Can I help you?" comes a voice.

I nearly jump out of my strappy gold sandals.

The voice is coming from a doorman wearing a dark-gray uniform (ooh, he matches the carpet). He's standing behind a marble desk.

"Um, yeah," I start. "I'm here to see Nadia Farouk."

"Top floor, Penthouse C," he says, and his right arm raises briefly to indicate the far wall.

Lifts. God, this is like a luxury hotel. I tip-tap across the dark-gray granite floor (yes, dark gray again, the people who designed this didn't have a lot of imagination), feeling awkward, sensing the doorman's eyes on my back. Wow, I'm already self-conscious. What's it going to be like at the party?

The lift door pings open. I press the button that reads PENTHOUSE. As the doors close, I turn to look at my reflection in the smoky mirrors that line the little cabin. My coat is old and a bit tight on me—the buttons are pulling over my chest. I take it off and drape it casually over my arm, so no one can see how manky it is (I forgot to buy a new one in preparation for this evening).

Okay, Scarlett, quick inventory.

Lips: sticky and red.

Eyes: tons of black eyeliner, shiny mauve eye shadow.

Cheeks: less blusher than the girl in the shop said to put on. I wiped half of it off as soon as I left when I caught sight of myself in a shop window and thought I had a red traffic light on either cheek.

Cover-up on incipient/fading spots (thank God no current ones): not too cakey. I think. It's hard to tell in the dim light. I put it on, blotted, and then put on more, just to be sure.

Nails: no chips on the varnish as far as I can—

Ping! The elevator bounces and stops moving.

And that's it. No more time. Gymnastics training allows me to spin round 180 degrees so fast that I don't think anyone could have noticed that I'd been checking myself out in the mirrors. I step out into the hallway. (You guessed it— dark-gray granite floors, dark-gray suede walls, etc., etc. There's a big vase of white orchids that probably cost more than my entire outfit standing on a table in front of me. And my outfit wasn't cheap.) No trouble telling which door is Penthouse C. The sexy R&B music is spilling out round the door frame, like water pouring through cracks. I push at the door. It's open.

Oh God. It's like *Teen Vogue* is staging a shoot in here. Sprawled all over the incredibly expensive leather sofas, sitting smoking on the lavish glass coffee tables, lounging against the walls, are what looks like the cream of London's teenage smart set. All self-consciously posed, knowing how decorative they are, as if they're just waiting for the photographer to purr that they're gorgeous and press the shutter button.

I stand there staring for a good minute or so, just taking it all in and trying not to hyperventilate. All I can hope for is that no one will look up, see me, point, and laugh. Plum's circle isn't exactly known for its generosity and friendliness. It's a bitch-eat-bitch world and you sink or swim by yourself.

Sorry about that mixed metaphor. My English teacher's eyes would pop out in fury if she caught that.

Thankfully, no one is pointing and laughing. At least not yet. I take a deep breath, knowing I can't just stand here all evening, when Nadia detaches herself from a huddle of young men who look like a boy band and rushes toward me.

"Scarlett!" she says. "I'm so glad you came!"

"Um, thanks," I say, amazed at her enthusiasm.

"Let me take your coat. Hang on, I'll be right back."

Nadia snatches my coat off my arm before I can say a word, and shoots off down a corridor. Without my coat to hold on to, I feel almost naked; there's nothing to do with my hands, and the front of my body is exposed. I suddenly understand why people smoke, though relieving social anxiety seems a high price to pay for lung cancer. I shift from foot to foot till Nadia returns.

"Now, we'll get you a drink," she says. "Let me show you to the bar."

Nadia sounds like she's been hosting parties all her life. She could be thirty-six instead of sixteen. And she looks much older than sixteen, too. She's as well groomed as a character from an American soap.

I follow Nadia through the room. People call her name and she smiles and waves, but keeps going. She's in a really thin phase—the school grapevine says she's running for hours every day and eating nothing but tuna in brine. It doesn't suit her, but there's no point telling her that. She'll just think I'm jealous and take it as a twisted compliment.

So I keep my mouth shut. Nadia is wearing a heavily embroidered white lacy blouse (over jeans, phew, I got that right) and the sleeves are full, which is good, as you can't see how terrifyingly skinny her arms are. If she tried to do a handstand, they'd buckle.

"Here's the bar," she says, gesturing.

I gulp. It really is a bar, with a whole array of bottles behind it on mirrored shelves, and ranks of glasses glistening under the built-in lighting refracting off the mirrors. There's even someone standing behind it, bending down to get something from a shelf below. My God, has Nadia actually hired a bartender?

"Wow," I gasp.

Nadia pushes at her flood of glossy black hair, which is hanging down her back. It's so heavy she has to pick it up with both hands to lift it and arrange it as she wants, draped over one shoulder. "I know! Isn't it utterly fabulous? My parents really love to entertain."

"They're not around, are they?" I ask.

She bursts out laughing. "God no! They're out of the country. Don't ask me where, I haven't bothered to look at the itinerary. What are you drinking? I'm on the fizz. Hey, Dan! More fizz!"

I jump at the name. But I don't turn my head to look for him, because that would be too obvious. As a result, when he straightens up from behind the bar, I find myself gazing into those wonderful eyes. I swallow hard.

"Hey," he says, grinning at me.

"Hey," I manage to reply.

"Scarlett," he says.

I expect Dan to add something else, but he doesn't. He just keeps grinning at me.

What the hell do I do now? Say his name back to him? That would be totally moronic, wouldn't it? Frantically, I scavenge around in every recess of my brain, trying to fish up some answer that isn't completely banal.

(Though part of me thinks that a boy just gazing at you and saying your name is pretty unfair, as it's an impossible thing to find a reply to.)

But all I can do is just gawk at Dan. His lips are really full, and I catch myself wondering whether they're as soft as they look. I know I'm blushing, but so what? It's not daylight in here, no one will notice. But someone's got to say something soon . . .

"Dan! Don't just *stand* there! More fizz, please!" Nadia commands, and waves a glass at him.

Dan turns to smile at her. Is it just my imagination, or is it hard for him to tear his gaze away from mine?

"Well, since I happen to be behind the bar," he says, reaching for a bottle of champagne.

At the sound of the cork popping, three incredibly sexy girls in backless dresses who are clustering farther down the bar start whooping. Dan fills flutes for me and Nadia and then, with an apologetic smile, walks down to refill the glasses of the backless chicks. I can't blame him, they're gorgeous. But it's horrible to watch him go.

"Stay right here," Nadia says to me. "I'm going to see if Simon's around. I know he wanted to say hi to you."

That's nice of Nadia, finding someone for me to talk to, I think, sitting down on a stool.

In the mirrors behind the bar, I can watch what's going on in the room. It's like a scene from a pop video. Shiny happy people, like that old R.E.M. song. There's a bowl of crisps in front of me on the bar, super-expensive blue designer ones. I definitely shouldn't have any (Ricky would kill me if he were watching), but nevertheless, I start nibbling on them. (Nibbling: a word often used as a euphemism for "shoving down one's throat as fast as possible.")

And my mind shifts into extreme overdrive. I begin asking myself pertinent questions, like: Why am I here? Why did Plum invite me? I've been wondering about that ever since Wednesday afternoon, and the only answer I can come up with is my father.

Titles are very important in the world of shiny happy people. In the mirror, I see Sophia Von und Zu Unpronounceable, perching on the arm of a sofa, throwing back her head, letting her long blond hair dangle down her back, and braying with laughter at some boy's joke. Sophia Von und Zu gets to hang out with the shiny happy people because she has a title. Sophia's in my history class, and I happen to know that she has the brain capacity of the donkey her laugh sounds like, and a considerably less interesting personality. She's really pretty, but that wouldn't have been enough to get her into Plum's inner circle. Her key to the door is the fact that she's a countess.

And so I assume that someone in Plum's entourage must have found out that my dad was Sir Richard Wakefield. Which means that I'm the daughter of a baronet. The title died out with my dad, because sexist rubbish British law says that only a boy can inherit a baronetcy, and I don't have any brothers (or sisters, for that matter). No more Wakefield baronetcy. But still, that must mean that they've decided that my heritage counts me as being posh enough to hang out with them. It wouldn't have been enough in itself, but it helps.

There are three main factors you need in order to be a part of Plum's group: poshness, money, and looks. Two out of three will probably get you in, if they're good enough. And I just barely scrape by on all three.

1. Daughter of a baronet. Poshness checked.

2. Small trust fund. Ditto re: money, though it's a pittance compared to what Nadia possesses.

3. Physical attractiveness. Well, this year was my growth spurt. In all the good directions. I grew a couple of inches, which made me look thinner. The gymnastics helped keep my weight down. And then there are the boobs. For the first time in my life, I look more like a woman than a girl.

Thinking about my figure has made me feel guilty about eating the crisps. I lick the grease off my fingers, deliberately not looking down the bar at Dan flirting with the backless girls. I'm not usually paranoid, and yet I don't quite trust all of this bounty. The champagne, the mirrors, the glittering people. I feel I'm being set up.

And I was. I just didn't realize how.

"Hey, sorry to abandon you."

It's Dan. Returned from pouring champagne for the backless girls. He's grinning at me. It's such a lovely smile that I would look behind me to see if there's someone else he's talking to, if it weren't for the fact that I can see clearly in the mirror that there isn't. Unless of course they're a vampire.

Scarlett! Focus!

"That's okay," I manage.

"I'm getting out of here. I don't want to get stuck bartending all evening."

Dan puts one hand on the bar top and vaults over it with impressive ease. Landing right in front of me. I'm close enough to distinguish the gray-green color of his eyes with no problem at all.

He reaches back to the bar and grabs another bottle of champagne. "It's sort of hot in here, isn't it? Want to go out on the terrace for a bit?"

I swallow hard. "There's a terrace?"

Dan laughs. "You've never been here before, have you?" he says, and it's not really a question. "Come on, I'll show you. Prepare to be impressed."

Dan holds out his other hand. I'm so unused to any kind of boy/girl stuff that it takes me a long time to realize that he wants me to take it. His palm is warm and dry, his fingers strong as they wrap around mine. Thank God I did my nails this morning.

That pang of relief doesn't last, though. Right now I want to run away. I want to disappear in a puff of smoke. I want Dan McAndrew never to let go of my hand.

Dan is leading me across the room to a pair of glass French doors. I follow him. What else can I do? If he'd asked me if I wanted to watch paint dry, I would have come with him and pretended that drying paint was the most interesting thing I ever saw in my life.

All of a sudden I start thinking about my New Year's wishes. I already got my breasts. Could this mean I'm going for number three?

Might I actually get to kiss Dan McAndrew?

I'm still clutching my champagne glass, and now I gulp down the rest of the contents as we walk. The thought of kissing Dan is so frightening that my entire lower body seems to be losing control of itself.

Please, God, don't let me make a fool of myself, I pray, more fervently than I've prayed for anything in my life. *Please, God . . .*

five
"SQUEEZE ME"

I don't make any sort of exclamation when Dan and I step out onto the terrace, but that's only because I can't think of words big enough to convey my amazement. It stretches away in the moonlight, so large I can barely see where it ends. There's a super-modern fountain in the center, a ribbon of water flowing over a granite loop. Topiary plants, those weird ones that snake up round a central wooden post, surround the outer wall, which, as far as I can tell, is made from sheets of glass.

The moon is nearly full, but even if it were pitch-dark outside, no problem, because, believe it or not, there's actually lighting set into the stone floor. Dan turns to see my reaction, and it's clearly all he hoped it would be. He bursts out laughing.

"Never fails to strike people dumb," Dan says as he leads me along one side of the fountain to a little recessed stone bench surrounded by more topiary.

"It's almost like being in a *garden*." I hike up my jeans a little before I sit down. "You'd never know it was a roof terrace."

"That's the point."

"Well, apart from the lights." I lift my feet to see the dim light emanating from under the bench more clearly.

Dan reaches for my glass and refills it. "Yeah, you generally don't get underfloor lighting in gardens."

"They must have *so much money*," I blurt out, and then I wince. Commenting on how much money people have is really vulgar. My grandmother would have a heart attack if she'd heard me say that.

But Dan doesn't seem offended. "That's why this place is party central. Nadia's parents are never here, and they don't care how much she spends on her parties, just as long as she doesn't bother them. Same old story, just with a ton of money, right?"

There's an edge to this I don't quite understand, but I nod as if I do, and sip more champagne.

"So how come I haven't seen you hanging out with them before?" Dan asks, shaking back his thick brown hair, so it's no longer falling in his face.

I'm sitting demurely, legs crossed, like a lady (I'm too nervous to relax at all), but Dan is straddling it in what I can't help feeling is a very manly way. His hands are pressed in front of him on the bench and he's leaning forward, so his face is close to mine. It's an overpowering sensation. I'm torn between simultaneous impulses to lean in and kiss him, and get up and flee. I almost think I'm going to get a cramp somewhere because the strain on my body is so extreme.

Dan is still looking at me with those captivating gray-green eyes, waiting for an answer.

"Um, I'm really busy a lot of the time with my gymnastics," I eventually say.

I don't want him to realize that I've only just been picked up by Plum and her set, like a toy they might have a craze for one day and forget all about the next. I don't want him to know that only in the last six months, when I shot up a couple of inches and sprouted curves, have I remotely looked like the kind of girl that Dan McAndrew might want to take out onto a terrace for a tête-à-tête.

"Oh yeah, that's right," Dan says. "You were in those workout clothes when I saw you the other day."

"Yeah, I was a bit sweaty," I say, utterly embarrassed. "I usually like to go and shower afterward, and then I have a lot of homework to do, so it's hard to come out much in the evenings. Gymnastics takes up a lot of time . . ."

God, I sound as if I'm a finalist in the Most Boring Teenager of All Time competition. Nice going, Scarlett. I sneak a look to see if Dan has nodded off to sleep, but he still looks interested. It's some sort of miracle.

"Gymnastics, wow," he says, his face lighting up a bit. "That's so cool. I'd love to try that."

I try to stifle a giggle, but I can't. "You're a bit old for anything serious now," I tell him. "You have to start really young if you want to do competitions."

Dan puts his hands on his hips in mock anger. "You don't think I'm strong enough? I do a ton of sports!"

I'm goggling at him, I know, but I can't stop, because

now he's rolling up one of his shirtsleeves to above the elbow. Dan flexes his arm and I swoon.

"Go on, feel!" he insists, flashing me his gorgeous smile. "Squeeze me!"

My cheeks feel hot and are probably as red as strawberries. Thank God it's dark out here. "Well, I would, but—"

"Go on, Scarlett. What are you afraid of?" Dan taunts me playfully.

When I think about how those backless girls would be all over him by now, I reach out my hand without any further hesitation and gingerly squeeze his forearm.

You'd think I would be familiar with the feel of a man's arm by now, after all the times Ricky has spotted me at gymnastics. But the sensations coursing through me are so different. Dan might be from a different species. His skin is velvety soft on the inside of his forearm, and the outer arm is lightly hairy, but the hairs are delicate, totally unlike Ricky's rough scratchy ones. I squeeze more. To be honest, after Ricky's bulging, gym-pumped muscles, Dan's are considerably less evident, but I can feel the strength there, and it makes me blush even harder. Electricity fizzes through me and my hand feels as though it's burning. I pull it back.

"See?" Dan says. "I could do gymnastics, right?"

"Um, yeah," I mumble.

It's difficult not to think about what other physical activities he's good at. I have to distract myself or I might have a mini fainting episode like I did at the fountain.

"That was a good vault you did over the bar," I say, inspiration striking me. I've heard that you should tell boys when they're good at physical stuff—they love that.

"Oh, I do stuff like that all the time," Dan says with a tinge of arrogance in his voice. It's really sexy.

"You've got good pop," I add.

Dan's brow furrows in confusion. "Good what?"

"Fast-twitch muscles," I explain. Now that I'm on my own ground, talking about stuff I know, I feel more at ease, which is why I swivel around to face him. "You need to have really fast reflexes to be good at gymnastics. Like when you land from a front handspring and just pop up in the air for a front somersault."

"Pop! I get it," Dan says, smiling widely. He's enjoying this, and I feel a rush of pride that we're having such a good conversation. "I bet you're really good, right?"

Oh my God, I think I just batted my eyelashes at him. "I'm okay," I reply, trying to be modest.

Dan doesn't buy it, though. "Come on, you train all the time. You must be really good."

"I've won some stuff," I admit. "Not major competitions or anything like that. I mean, I'll never make the nationals."

Dan's eyebrows arch up. "You've got medals?"

I smirk a bit at the memory of winning second place for the floor exercise a couple years ago. "Some trophies."

"Hey, show me something!" Dan asks, his eyes shining.

"What?"

"Show me some gymnastics. Go on!"

I stare at him, dumbfounded. "It's *dark*. There's a *stone floor*. I've been *drinking*."

61

"Ohhhh." Dan does a sort of boy-pout. His lips look wonderful when he does that, all full and luscious. "There must be *something* you could do," he says persuasively.

For a split second I actually consider trying to pull off two back handsprings on a stone floor after two glasses of champagne. I want to impress him that much. Then I roll my eyes at my own idiocy. God, the things we'll do to show off for people we're mad keen on.

Dan's still staring at me, those gray-green eyes huge and beautiful. He blinks momentarily, and his feathery eyelashes seem long enough to brush against his cheekbones. He's impossible to refuse.

I sigh, kick off my sandals, and give him my glass to hold. "Woo-hoo!" he cheers.

My jeans are fairly tight, so I have to be careful. But I just realized that I don't need to do anything that difficult. Dan won't have the faintest idea what's really hard and what isn't. I stand up, flash him a smile (now that I'm performing I have all the confidence in the world, I'm so used to it) and lunge forward, kicking up to a handstand.

Dan hoots and claps gleefully, the idiot. Like this is even hard. I settle into the handstand and sink my back into enough of an arch to let me move. And then I start walking. Down the length of the terrace for ten feet or so; 180-degree turn, back arching just a bit more to pull that off. Walk back down again to where I started, hands sore from the cracks in the stone pavement. Right in front of the bench, I do a full 360-degree turn, front-splitting my legs for full effect. Dan is applauding like mad now. I bring my legs straight up, drop back into bridge, and stand upright. Ow, that last bit was too ambitious with the champagne in my system. I feel a bit sick and dizzy. I wobble on the balls of my feet before I get full balance. I am so not used to drinking.

But Dan is too busy cheering to notice.

"That was *amazing!*" he says with such enthusiasm I feel a huge wave of pride, even though I've been doing hand-stand walks since I was nine.

"Scarlett? My God, that was *so good!*"

Another male voice echoes in the night air. I swivel around and find myself looking at pink-and-white Simon, wearing a blue blazer and jeans, his blond hair slicked back. He looks quite good all dressed up, but I almost laugh because he's goggling at me as if I'd just turned into a cartoon version of myself.

"Hey, Simon," Dan says, and he's clearly not happy to see him. "Show's over, mate."

"I know you said you did gymnastics, Scarlett, but that was *incredible!*" Simon compliments me, and although what I did was bog-standard in my world, I'm still flattered by his sheer, friendly enthusiasm.

"Thanks," I say, mindlessly wiping my hands on my brand-new jeans.

"Venetia said she saw you going out onto the terrace, so I thought I'd find you and say hi," Simon explains.

"Well, you've found her, and she's busy," Dan interrupts. "Take a number."

Simon stuffs his hands in his pockets, obviously embar-rassed. "Oh, am I interrupting? Sorry, I didn't mean—"

"Scarlett, we need to toast your gymnastic skills!" Dan cuts off Simon's apology. He's refilled our glasses and now he holds them up, offering one to me.

"I'm sort of hanging out with Dan at the moment," I say to Simon, equally embarrassed.

"Right, right, yeah, got it . . ."

Simon backs away. I think he keeps backing right through the French doors and into the flat again, but I don't see him go, because I'm walking over to Dan to take the glass he's holding out to me. He watches me all the way, and normally that would make me utterly self-conscious, but my success at the hand-stand walk, coupled with the fact that now I'm barefoot, which is a state in which I feel confident, helps so much that I actually manage a sort of sexy swing of the hips as I approach him.

I take the glass. I clink it against his. I gaze up into his eyes and smile. He's really tall now that my sandals are off.

"You're tiny," he says, reading my mind. "I could pick you up in the palm of my hand."

Wow, he thinks I'm tiny! Podgy, stomach-muffin me, with my thirty-four Ds and my big round bum! I melt toward him (literally), and the next thing I know, Dan is taking the glass from me and putting both of them down on the bench. And then he turns around and pulls me toward him, and my face is tilting up toward his as if an invisible hand was tug-ging it back, and I can feel his arms around my back, and his head comes down really slowly.

I feel his warm breath on my face. His chest presses hard against mine, flattening my breasts, which makes me feel really embarrassed about them. He nudges my head sideways so he can reach my mouth without our noses getting in the way, and I think *Oh, so that's how it's done . . .*

And then his lips are gently pressing against mine. They're really soft. I don't know what I was expecting. I've never kissed anyone on the mouth before. Sixteen and never been kissed. God, how tragic. I'm terrified of doing it wrong. At least I've seen a ton of kisses on TV and in films. What did people do before television? How did they have any idea what it meant to kiss someone properly? You can read about stuff in books, but that's nothing compared to seeing it happen.

It's part of going to an all-girls' school, of course: if I'd been at a normal, mixed school, I'd have snogged at least a few boys by now. But then this wouldn't be my first kiss. With Dan. On this terrace. With a soft night breeze lifting my hair, and stars in the sky. So I'd rather have it this way. And it's not as if he's pulled away, laughing at me and telling me I obviously don't know what I'm doing . . .

God, Scarlett! Where is your brain going? I'm so dazed with what's happening I feel like I'm on drugs, or drunk, or both. I feel as light as a feather (dizzy and spinning with the sensation of Dan's lips on mine and the extraordinary concept that it's me, out of all the girls here, that he wants to kiss) and as heavy as lead (I'm gigantic, I must weigh twenty pounds more than Plum, how can he bear to touch me?). Dan's hand is on my waist and I'm terrified that it will (a) stray down and feel the fat on my side, or (b) stray up and touch my breast, which would make me scared that he's only kissing me because of them, but he's kissing me and kissing me and I'm kissing him back and suddenly I can't think of anything but his mouth.

They say "kissed," but really it's hundreds of tiny kisses. You don't see that so much on TV. I wasn't expecting this: Dan is kissing all around my lips, till they feel swollen, big and pouty like a supermodel's. And now he's nipping at them, biting them lightly, but somehow that's incredibly exciting. I feel something inside me melt and pour like honey, and I realize that I'm nipping back at him, teasing him with little bites like he's teasing me. He groans. That's a little scary, because he sounds like a man when he makes that sound. It comes from deep down inside him, like the part of me that's melting.

And then Dan wraps his arms around me tightly, and his tongue slides into my mouth, warm and wet.

I knew this was going to happen. But I thought I would have to brace myself, because it would feel weird, and instead it feels *unbelievably sexy*. It's the sexiest thing I have ever felt in my life. I hear someone moaning and I realize that it's me, and Dan's making that deep groaning noise again and clutching me to him, and I'm clinging on to him for dear life, and my tongue is meeting his.

We're entwined like someone's roped our bodies tightly together. We're holding on to each other like we'll drown if we let go. I can't imagine ever wanting this to stop.

And then the terrible thing happens, and nothing will ever be the same again.

six

"YOU KILLED HIM"

All of a sudden, Dan's grasp loosens. He jerks back from me so abruptly that cold air rushes in on the front of my body. My hands drop, too. I feel stupid, holding on to him when he's let go of me. I must have done something that showed him how inexperienced I was. He's probably embarrassed that he ever wanted to kiss me in the first place.

However, that fear drifts away and another takes its place when I see that Dan's hands are scrabbling at his jeans pocket. His skin is losing its color and his eyes are fixed on me, like he's in a state of sheer panic. He manages to gasp out some sounds that resemble words.

Oh my God. Now I realize that he's choking—

"_Scarlett_," he manages, clawing at his pocket. "_Help me . . ._"

Inside my head, I'm screaming. _What did I do wrong?_

Dan staggers backward. He's wheezing and clutching at his chest. When his legs buckle underneath him, the scream inside my head finally comes out of my mouth.

I run toward Dan and catch him just as he's about to

knock his head on the bench, and I lower him to the ground. It's even harder to make sure he doesn't crash and hit himself, because he doesn't put his hands out to brace his fall, or cling to me: his hands have moved up to his throat. And when I've got my breath back, because six feet of teenage boy is not a light weight to support in your arms, I scream over and over again.

But the music is loud inside, and everyone's laughing. I banish any embarrassment I might feel at shoving my hands in Dan's pockets and dive in to see what he was looking for, if there's something that might fix whatever's going on with him. And I keep screaming at the top of my lungs, screaming till my throat's raw and painful.

But by the time Simon hears me only a bare couple of minutes later, and comes running out to see what's going on, it's too late.

Dan has suffocated to death in my arms.

* * *

After that, everything's a blur of movement and confusion and screaming and bright lights stabbing through the dark . . .

An ambulance parking at the front of the building, its blue swiveling light sweeping round and round, casting ghostly flashes up against the glass of the terrace, streaking across the plants, throwing eerie flashes of blue lightning across Dan's face, across the paramedics bending down by his lifeless body, across my hands as they pry them loose from him and pull me away from his corpse . . .

Someone screaming like a maniac, wild and grieving and raucous. Not me. I've screamed my throat dry and I can barely speak . . .

A paramedic holding me by the upper arms, her hair scraped back so tightly from her forehead that the skin looked stretched, the dark-blue eyeliner rimming her eyes, the sharp tone of her voice asking insistently over and over again what happened, if I saw Dan take anything, anything at all? But I didn't. I don't know what happened. And my voice is gone, so I just keep shaking my head, back and forth back and forth, until she says something about being in shock, and pushes me down on the bench and shoves my head down between my legs so I don't faint . . .

Simon, rushing to my side, asking me if I'm all right, sounding so concerned it makes me burst into tears and the paramedic shoos him away . . .

And Plum. Bursting through throngs of people, including Simon and the paramedic, yelling at me, "You killed him!" she screams. "You killed him!" I think Simon tries to say something to her, but she shoves him away. And she's more than a match for the paramedic—she shoves her away, too, and keeps screaming at me: "You killed him, you *bitch*!" until finally the police come and take her away and soon I'm being taken away, too, out through the doors of Nadia's apartment, down the elevator, into a car, and speeding off to God knows where . . .

"Did you bring anything to the party, Scarlett?" the older policeman asks me. "You know what I mean, don't you? Something to get things going, liven you up a bit?"

I stare at him, completely confused. I'm cold. They didn't bring my coat. I don't care about my coat, it was falling to pieces and too small for me anyway, but my arms are bare and feel like ice.

"I don't think Scarlett understands what you're asking," says Lady Severs coldly. "And frankly no more do I."

She's not in the best of moods, having been woken up and summoned to Knightsbridge police station so that the authorities can have an adult present when they formally question me. I didn't realize they were going to ring her: they asked for my home phone number and twenty minutes later Lady Severs, wearing her usual tweed suit, sensible walking shoes, and disapproving frown, stalked into the waiting room. They must have sent a car for her.

The older policeman taps a pencil on the table and looks at his partner, who looks no more than twenty-one.

"Or something to relax you?" suggests the young police-man, smiling at me in such a friendly way it's almost confus-ing, like we've met before and I just don't remember. "You know, take the edge off? Lots of people do it."

I shake my head, dumb from misery and incomprehension. They exchange glances again.

"You won't get in trouble if you tell the truth, Scarlett," says the older policeman, and that does actually make me snort a bit. How moronic does he think I am? I mean, *three-year-olds* know that's the biggest lie of all!

They must have misinterpreted my snort, because the older one's eyes narrow into nasty slits, as does his mouth.

"All right, young lady," he says, and his voice is now as menacing as a bad cop in American TV shows. "If that's the way you want to do things, fine with me. I think you know we're talking about illegal substances. What did you take to the party and give to Dan McAndrew when you were alone with him on the terrace? You'd better tell me right now, or you'll be in even worse trouble."

I gape at him, unable to believe what I'm hearing. Why would I ever want to hurt Dan? But then it dawns on me that these two men know nothing about my feelings for Dan. And I can't tell them, because if I do I'll burst into tears and never be able to stop.

"It was the first time you'd been asked to a party at Nadia Farouk's, wasn't it?" the younger policeman chips in. All pretend-friendliness has vanished: his tone's equally un-pleasant now. "You weren't part of their crowd, were you? So why did they ask you along? Because you had something they wanted? Were you their new dealer? Come on, Scarlett, don't piss around with us."

I'm goggling at them. It's really upsetting to have two police officers say such horrible things to you, with such nasty looks in their eyes, but their words are so far removed

71

from any reality that I still can't believe I'm hearing them. I know they want me to answer, but I'm so gobsmacked by what they're suggesting that I'm tongue-tied. Which is not a bad thing, as Lady Severs is already jumping into the gap.

"What kind of language is that?" she demands furiously. "How *dare* you speak that way in my presence? And to suggest that *Scarlett* would— I've never heard anything so ridiculous and insulting in my life!"

"With respect, your ladyship," says the older policeman, leaning toward her, "adults often have no idea what the kids in their charge are really getting up to."

"My good man," interrupts Lady Severs, in a voice so cold you could get frostbite from it, "I know *exactly* what Scarlett, as you put it, 'gets up to.' Scarlett is a gymnast. She trains every day after school with her two friends. Then she goes round to one or the other's house to do her homework. I know that because, as arranged with her grandmother, a very dear friend of mine, one or other of the parents rings me to confirm that fact. She is always home by ten p.m. and goes straight up to her room. On the evenings that she does not see her friends, she is in her room doing her homework. There are very strict rules under which Scarlett is allowed to stay in my house, and I make sure she abides by them. She has to hand her mobile phone to me every night when she comes in, and retrieve it the next morning, to ensure that she doesn't stay up late jabbering with her friends."

It's the policemen's turn to stare, speechless, at Lady Severs.

"She might have another mobile you don't know about . . . ," starts the older one, but you can tell his heart isn't in it. Lady Severs waves a hand at him dismissively, and he falls silent.

"Scarlett's parents died when she was very young," she continues, with so little feeling in her voice that it's as if she were telling them what time it was. "She is the ward of her grandmother, and I agreed to put Scarlett up in my house during term-time on the strict condition that she would obey a system of behavior I deemed appropriate for a girl of her age. Any deviation of those rules, and she would no longer be welcome. She has kitchen access during specific hours of the day, and her own bathroom. And up till now, I must say, she has been very little trouble, all things considered."

Both policemen turn and look at me. There's silence for quite a while. Then the younger policeman holds up an index finger to the older one in a "hold on" gesture, gets up from his chair, and leaves the room. We sit there, saying nothing, till he returns. He's holding a polystyrene cup, which he slides across the table to me. Hot tea with milk. I'm really grateful. I blow on it and take a sip. It's got a lot of sugar in it, which picks me up a little bit. And it makes talking easier, even though it hurts to swallow.

The policemen, despite themselves, are looking at me with pity now. Strangely, I dislike that even more than when they were doing the bad-cop interrogation routine. Pity's worse than anything. Just ask an orphan—they'll tell you that.

Great. How tragic is it to have *policemen* feeling sorry for you because you're a pathetic orphan with the social life of roadkill? I almost preferred it when they were thinking I was some kind of drug dealer. Still, I do want them to believe that the last thing in the world I wanted was to harm Dan.

God, I can't believe he's . . . gone. Tears prick at my eyelids. I shove the awful memory away. I'll cry later. When I'm alone.

"How did you get permission to go to the party, Scarlett?" the older one asks, quite nicely now.

"Scarlett told me that she had been invited by the Saybourne girl," Lady Severs answers. "A very good family. I see nothing wrong with the occasional socially acceptable gathering, once a month or so. Scarlett had a curfew, of course."

The only thing Lady Severs didn't know was that the party was unsupervised. A small detail that I conveniently left out. Only now I wish that Lady Severs had forbidden me to go. That way, none of us would be here.

And Dan might still be alive.

"Scarlett," the younger policeman says. "You're sure you didn't see Dan take anything?"

I shake my head. My whole body feels so heavy, I feel like I'm sinking.

"No. The paramedic kept asking me that, but he didn't do anything but drink a bit of champagne. He kept scrabbling in his pockets, though, when he was . . . when he was choking."

I'm about to cry, so I have to stop talking. I stare down at my tea, squeezing the polystyrene to make the liquid into an oval shape, distracting myself so the tears won't come again.

"He had severe allergies, apparently," the younger one says. "You weren't aware of that?"

"No," I murmur. "But I hardly knew him."

"You hardly knew him, but you were outside on the terrace with him, alone?" asks the younger policeman curiously.

"We were just talking," I mumble.

He looks at his notes and follows his writing with his index finger. "You told the paramedic that you were kissing when he started to choke."

Lady Severs turns to stare at me, making a loud, disapproving tutting sound with her tongue. The blood rushes to my face. Oh God, this is so awful. Why don't they just write MURDEROUS SLUT on my forehead with a marker? They might as well. Plum will do it as soon as I go back to school.

Dan's life is over, and my life is ruined. Feelings of misery are swallowing me whole. The older policeman has to repeat his next question before I take it in.

"Did you see Dan with a kind of glass tube? Like a thermometer, but bigger?"

"No," I say blankly.

The policemen exchange glances. I wonder if this is some drug reference I'm not cool enough to get.

"The lab results haven't come back yet, but one of our theories is that Dan may have died of an allergic reaction," the older policeman explains. "Apparently, he always carried something called an EpiPen, so he could inject himself in case he had a possibly fatal reaction to something. That could have been what he was looking for in his pocket. However, it wasn't on him, and we canvassed the apartment and didn't turn up anything there either."

"What could he have been allergic to?" I ask.

"That's the mystery, isn't it?" says the first policeman. "We're trying to establish that. Definitive test results will most likely take weeks."

Lady Severs clicks her tongue again and gathers her coat around her, a clear sign that she's ready to leave. "So, to summarize, this unfortunate young man had some sort of allergic reaction, had been foolish enough not to bring his remedy with him, and dropped dead at Scarlett's feet. I fail to see why she should be involved in this interrogation a moment longer."

"Like we said before, my lady, it's just one of our theories. Once the labs come back, we'll have real clues as to what happened. Either way, she'll have to testify at the inquest, I'm afraid," the older policeman says.

Lady Severs gasps in dismay.

"Surely that's not necessary!" she protests.

"I'm sorry, my lady. In any case of suspicious death like this, an inquest is mandatory."

The older policeman gives me a long dubious stare. He may have given up the notion that I'm a drug dealer, but it's quite obvious that he's convinced I'm somehow responsible for Dan's death.

I shiver, remembering Plum screaming at me

He's not the only one who thinks that.

"The *publicity*!" Lady Severs recoils from me, staring down her nose as if I'm what she would call a "common person" who's dared to talk back to her. It's her worst look of all.

Now that the initial shock of Dan's collapse and death is draining away, now that I have some sweet milky tea inside me, the terrible truth of the situation is beginning to take hold of me. I've lost practically everything that made my life worth living: my old friends, my new acquaintances, my room in Holland Park (because I really doubt Lady Severs will let me go on living there, now that I've dragged her down to the Knightsbridge police station in the middle of the night and caused a huge scandal).

And Dan. I've lost anything that might have happened between me and Dan.

I remember his kiss, and tears come to my eyes.

It's not just the policemen who think I might have caused Dan's death. Plum did, too, and by now so will everyone else. Though I can't remotely think of anything I could have done that could have hurt Dan, I was the last person to see him alive.

If the tests and the inquest don't determine what killed him, every single person who knows about Dan's death is going to assume that I'm to blame.

And the worst part is that so will I.

PART TWO: A.D.

"It wasn't your fault."

I sit and look at those words for a long time. I want to write more, I really do.

But I'm scared.

I pick up my pen and start to scribble over the sentence, canceling it out. Years ago I learnt that to cover up words properly, you write other words on top of them, so that no one can squint and see the letters hiding underneath. So I write over the top. Again and again, till you can't make out a single letter, just a tangled mass of black ink.

I put down my pen and stare at the paper. And then I realize that, without meaning to, I've used the same sentence that I wanted to conceal. I've written the same words over and over again, like those old-fashioned films where the teacher makes a schoolkid keep writing a sentence on a blackboard till the whole surface is filled with white chalk.

"It wasn't your fault," I've written.

"It wasn't your fault."

It wasn't your fault."

I pick up the piece of paper and scrunch it up with my hand and throw it in the bin. Where it joins a crumpled-up mass of other papers, all with the same black mass scribbled on them, which is those same words written again and again and again. . . .

And I hate myself. Because I'm a coward. Because I'm not brave enough to look at those words on the page without canceling them out again straightaway.

I'm a coward. And right now I wish I was dead. Because this secret is much too big for me to be able to keep.

seven

A FRESH NEW START

"The most important thing," my grandmother says, "is that you put the past behind you. You mustn't dwell. What can't be cured must be endured."

It's all I can do to stop my eyes from rolling up in their sockets. You know, it's much harder than you'd think to control your eyeballs. They're used to moving without any conscious effort of the brain. How often do you have to tell your eyes to do something? Think how many times you tell your stomach to suck itself in. You never do that with your eyes, do you?

In an effort not to make a crazed face, I fix my stare on my grandmother till my eyes start watering. I've heard this speech from her hundreds of times before. Don't dwell, pluck up, what-can't-be-cured, etc., etc. Ever since my mother and father died—over a decade ago. And no matter how much she says it, it never helps.

"You've had the summer to let things settle," my grandmother continues. "A few months."

"Barely three," I mumble.

"What, Scarlett?" my grandmother says impatiently. "Speak up. You know I can't abide muttering."

"Three months," I say as I tug on the hem of my black sweater. "It's barely been three months since . . . "

I still can't say the words out loud: "since Dan died."

My grandmother waves her hand. "More than enough time," she says imperiously, commanding me with both the tone of her voice and her gesture to agree with her. "No dwelling, Scarlett. It stops you from achieving your goals. And stop fidgeting. It's a nasty habit."

There's a loud knock on the door.

"Come!" my grandmother calls with the authoritative tone of the Queen Mother.

I don't know why she doesn't add "in," but I've heard her say that single word so often that I take it for granted. Grandmother doesn't run a bath, she "draws" it. She doesn't drink tea, she "takes" it. All very old-fashioned, aristocratic English, the kind of thing you can really only get away with if you're—

"Lady Wakefield? Your tea," says her perfectly groomed assistant Penelope, entering the room with the afternoon tea tray. Silver teapot, white bone china Minton cups, matching plate with plain dry tea biscuits.

"Scarlett?" my grandmother, Lady Wakefield, says. "Will you pour?"

My eyes want to start rolling once again. Grandmother is always trying to "make a lady of me." I feel like an idiot lifting that big silver teapot—it's like something out of a period film. But then, that's how my grandmother lives. I look around her study, with its paneled mahogany walls and polished antique furniture. On the walls are paintings of our ancestors, including a Victorian Lady Wakefield in the appropriate corset and crinoline. It's like a time capsule in here.

I manage to direct the stream of pale tea into the cups without too much spillage. Behind me, Penelope coughs politely.

"Lady Wakefield?" she says. "I'm so sorry, Scarlett—it's just, you know, the start of a new year—so much to get on with—time is pressing . . . "

I don't think I've ever heard Penelope finish a sentence. She always gives the impression of being much too busy to get one out.

"Absolutely!" my grandmother says. "Scarlett, my dear, drink up your tea. You know what things are like in September. Terribly busy. Complete insanity."

I nod, and pour us each a drop of milk from the milk jug. I prefer my tea very strong, with lots of milk and sugar, but according to Grandma that's for the common folk. People as posh as us "take" their tea very weak, with barely any milk. Her task accomplished, Penelope slips discreetly from the room.

"You know the drill around here, of course," my grandmother says, her lips pursing tightly.

I resort to wringing my hands behind my back. "Well, yes and no."

"So I don't need to go over it as I would for other girls," she continues on as if she hasn't heard me. "I must say, I wish it hadn't come to this."

"I don't want to be here either," I interject.

"I certainly didn't think it was a good idea for you to come here. It would not have been my choice. That's why I arranged for you to go to St. Tabitha's, and boarded you with Lady Severs, who, I must say, was *not* as understanding as she could have been about this situation." My grandmother sighs. "Still, neither she nor I are as young as we were, and I certainly wouldn't like those vulgar photographers pestering me like horseflies whenever I tried to leave my own house. But needs must as the devil drives. And after the death of that young boy . . . "

One thing about my grandmother: she always calls a spade a spade. No beating around the bush for her.

"I quite understand the headmistress of St. Tabitha's deciding that it would be best for you to make a fresh start at a new school. No headmistress would appreciate the press camped outside the school gates for the rest of the summer term. And apparently there were a lot of anonymous letters and e-mails. Teenage girls!" She sighs. "They can be very cruel, can't they?"

I don't bother to agree. I just sip my tea and try not to think about the contents of my e-mail in-box. Or the fact that I've had to change my mobile phone number and cancel all my IM accounts. No one knows better than I do how cruel teenage girls can be.

"So here we are," says my grandmother with a sigh. "A fresh start. Term begins tomorrow. We'll just have to draw a line under the incident and make the best of the situation, won't we?"

She gives me her famous smile, which basically means that you're dismissed from the room. My grandmother is as smartly turned out as ever. Pearls round her neck and clipped to her ears—they'll come to Aunt Gwen when she dies, but I don't think Aunt Gwen's expecting to clasp that pearl necklace at her throat any time soon. Hair as white as her pearls in a neatly trimmed bob. Blue eyes bright and clear as periwinkles, and as all-seeing as satellite radar. Not a trace of makeup on her face apart from a little powder and some pale pink lipstick.

I get up and bend over to kiss her goodbye. Her cheek is soft, tissue paper over velvet.

"I'm sure you'll have a very happy time with us, Scarlett," she says.

"Yes, Grandma," I say, walking toward the door.

"Oh, that reminds me." My grandmother turns in her chair. Its high tapestry back means she has to crane round it to see me, but she manages to make even this movement seem elegant. "It should be Lady Wakefield in term time, not Grandma," she says. "Very awkward for everyone if protocol isn't observed, I think. And the same for your aunt Gwen."

"Yes, *Lady Wakefield*," I say sarcastically, and shoot out of the door before she can reprimand me for my tone of voice.

I stand there in the corridor for a few moments. My grandmother's suite of rooms are kept up like the old days, with antique furnishings—the big gilt-framed mirror hanging over the occasional table, the leather chairs on either side, set up for parents and their daughters waiting for an interview in the Holy of Holies, Grandmother's study. You'd think it was still a stately home. Only one little thing gives it away. The brass plaque on the door, which reads:

HEADMISTRESS'S STUDY. ENTER ONLY UPON INVITATION.

*   *   *

The girls aren't allowed to use the central mahogany staircase, with its two wings flowing round the sides of the Great Hall. Grandma is too worried that hordes of running schoolgirl feet will wear the precious old wood down to nothing. Only teachers can use it. And me, when it's not term time. After official interviews with Grandma, I used to take the steps two at a time, eager to get away as fast as possible. But today I just walk down them slowly. Why hurry? It's not as if there's anything left in my life I'm remotely excited about. No need to rush toward nothing.

More oil paintings line the paneled walls of the Great Hall. There's a giant tapestry hanging in the gallery, where the two wings of the staircase begin their descent. It's an odd combination of medieval and Victorian, built that way by nineteenth-century Wakefields who liked the romance of living in medieval times—Knights! Jousting! Um, eating without cutlery and throwing the bones to the dogs!—but didn't have an ancestral home that dated back to the thirteenth century. They had to build their own, on a large estate which, at that time, was well away from the stinky metropolis of London.

And they did a ridiculously thorough job of it. Wakefield Hall sprawls on and on for miles, and that's just the house. The landscaping is pretty extensive, too: there's a hedge maze, a lime-tree walk, formal terraces on the southwest side, and weeping willows and even an ornamental lake (now fenced off for safety reasons). The house itself kept being added on to, as the original Sir Henry Wakefield, pumped up with excitement about having been made a baronet and given a ton of land by Queen Victoria, simply couldn't stop adding wings onto it.

There are parts of it that are walled off and we never enter—unsuitable for schoolrooms. Ironically, when my grandmother realized that nobody apart from a billionaire could afford to live in Wakefield Hall—the heating costs alone are enough to pay off the Third World debt—and decided to make it into a school, she had to build a whole new prefab wing round the back. Plus the gymnasium. And the swimming pool. And the tennis and netball courts. It's a small country here, really. Or at least a county.

Grandmother's been running Wakefield Hall Collegiate for nearly fifty years. Imagine spending half a century at school.

And right now it feels as if that's what I've been condemned to. An eternity at Wakefield Hall.

I push open one of the huge main double doors, each of which weighs roughly as much as a small car. They're wedged open in term time from seven-thirty to nine a.m., for the teachers and sixth-formers to use. Two good things about being in the sixth form: you get to wear your own clothes and use the main door. The first one, of course, being a lot more important. I think there was a rebellion ten years ago—girls in their last two years of school were humiliated by having to travel on the tube in those awful brown Wakefield Hall uniforms. I mean, it's all right when you're twelve, but being seventeen and eighteen and still wearing a school uniform—you'd be a total laughingstock. Not to mention an easy target for every mugger around.

Outside it's warm and breezy, a lovely sunny September day, enough to cheer up anyone whose life hadn't come to a screaming halt three months ago, when she was accused of killing someone and had no way to prove anyone wrong, including herself.

I kick the gravel as I wander down the drive. There's a huge stone fountain in the middle of it, not working, however. Little girls used to dare each other to come out here (playing on the drive is obviously strictly forbidden) and splash the water over each other. Grandmother didn't like that one little bit. So the leaping stone dolphins don't dribble water out of their mouths into the stone bowls being held by the fat little stone angels (I know, it doesn't make much sense—what are angels doing in a fountain?). There's something very sad about a fountain with no water in it. Mind you, everything seems sad to me at the moment.

It's half a mile down the drive to the house where I'm staying. Technically, it's my home, but I can't bring myself to call it that. Though it must be home: I read a sentence once that said something like "home is the place where they have to take you in," and that indeed is a good description of my aunt Gwen's little nook.

Aunt Gwen had to take me in when I was four, and my parents died in a motorbike crash. She didn't want to do it then, and she doesn't want to do it now. I was over the moon about getting out of here to go and live at Lady Severs's charming abode, but Aunt Gwen was ecstatic. She couldn't chuck me out the door fast enough. And now I'm back, like a bad penny. Having killed someone. Aunt Gwen must think she's cursed.

Well, she wouldn't be the only one.

We live in the gatehouse, which, as one can sort of tell from the name, is directly by the main entrance gates, which are enormous and imposing, designed to intimidate anyone visiting Wakefield Hall. The gatehouse is a stone cottage, and the gatekeeper and his family lived here in the old days, opening the gate for visitors in return for free accommodation.

If it seems a bit weird that my grandmother lives in full baronet-ial splendor up at the Hall, and my Aunt Gwen only gets the stone cottage that one of the lesser servants used to have, well, it seems odd to me, too. Aunt Gwen justifies it by saying that she "likes some space from Mother," which would make sense if you didn't know that there are a ton of other buildings on the Wakefield Hall estate that aunt Gwen could have, most of them not on the road, and a lot bigger. Like the one my dad had, before he and my mum moved to London. My dad was the favored child. My aunt Gwen got the short straw. I feel sorry for her about that—or I would, if she didn't take it out on me.

School starts in five days. I might as well go over my holiday work. I'm a bit behind: after Dan died, I missed a few weeks of school.

I couldn't have gone back to St. Tabby's as a student. I did briefly sneak in there once, to clear out my locker, and Plum and her entourage practically kicked me to death with their stilettos and wrote swear words all over my broken corpse. Even for that visit to St. Tabby's, they had to sneak me in by the service entrance, because the press was waiting outside the school, hoping to take a photo of me. They had to take me out of Lady Severs's house for the inquest with my head under a blanket, because that was under siege by photographers, too. Lady Severs was so furious I thought her head was going to spin round and round in fury, like that girl in *The Exorcist*. My life for that fortnight, trapped in that house with her, was like being in solitary confinement with one very angry warder with a big grudge against you.

After the whole inquest fuss was over—after it became clear that nothing had been resolved by the verdict—Aunt

Gwen came and got me and smuggled me out to a car in the middle of the night and brought me here. Wakefield Hall's giant iron gates clanged shut behind the car.

They just transferred me from one prison to another.

At least in this one I'm not trapped in my bedroom all the time. I get the run of the grounds. But I still have a jailer who's taken against me. Unhappy as I am to be back in the gatehouse of Wakefield Hall, believe me, Aunt Gwen is ten times unhappier about having me here full-time.

I used to be able to avoid coming back here by staying with Luce and Alison for the holidays. But that's not an option anymore. Speaking of which, I've tried to ring Luce and Alison on several occasions, but they wouldn't talk to me. Their phones went straight to voice mail.

I don't blame them. I wouldn't talk to me either.

The noise I'm making as I walk along, sullenly digging my toes into the gravel and churning it up, is loud in the quiet of the afternoon. Maybe that's why I'm doing it, just to have something to listen to. Wakefield Hall is always like a ghost village when it's not full of girls' voices screaming, bells ringing, and the whistles of PE teachers.

And the crackle must be loud enough to have attracted someone else's attention. A head pops up from behind a big lavender bush, one of a whole row that runs along one side of the drive. I jump with surprise, and skid slightly (and embarrassingly) on the gravel.

"Sorry if I startled you," the head says.

I glare at it with contempt. "You *did* startle me," I snap.

"What do you think you're doing, skulking around behind a bush like that?"

The head moves, and the rest of its body comes into view—or most of it, as the middle part is still partly concealed by the rounded side of the lavender bush. It's a man—or, now I look at him more closely, no, it isn't. Though his voice is deep, he's actually more a boy. Probably only a few years older than me. Tall, broad-shouldered, but with that teenage-boy leanness that means he doesn't have that much flesh on his bones yet. Beyond that, I barely take in what he looks like, because I'm deliberately not looking at his face. Boys are off-limits to me from now on. I'm basically trying to pretend they don't exist.

He holds up a pair of what I think are called secateurs, and I notice as he does so that while he's not exactly bulky, his forearms are veined with muscle. Which means he must be pretty strong.

"I was trimming the lavender," he says, a bit unnecessarily, but considering my grumpiness, he probably feels the need to overexplain. "And then I heard you coming down the drive, and I thought, *That must be a girl, cuz teachers don't kick gravel like that.* Not in my experience, anyway. So I was curious and I popped my head up to see who it was, because term hasn't started yet."

"Well, now you've satisfied your curiosity," I say flatly.

"Not really," he says, looking straight into my eyes. There must be a flash of sunlight on his face as he does that, because his eyes seem golden. It's a weird optical illusion, but . . . wow, it's so striking, especially added to the fact that he's staring at me, that I have to duck my head.

I can't look directly at him. Even this simple little conversation is overloading my brain. God, I am so messed up.

"You're Scarlett, aren't you?" he asks, but he doesn't wait for me to answer. "Couldn't mistake you. There's a picture in the Great Hall that could be you, a girl wearing a dress and one of those crown things."

"Tiaras," I say.

"Yeah. You're a Wakefield, all right. No mistaking that. Back living here, then? You were away in London, weren't you?"

Every question he asks is like a file grating directly onto my skin, cutting me raw. Which is odd, because he has a really nice voice, deep and warm.

"You must be bored here after London, eh? Can't be much for you to do round here."

"I'm fine," I say shortly, and because I can see he's about to add yet another comment on how boring and sad my life is, I turn away and keep walking down the drive.

"See you later!" he calls after me.

Not if I can help it, I want to shout back.

I can barely cope with talking to a boy, let alone one who seems like he might be remotely interested in getting to know me. How can I even think about boys? The only one I ever kissed dropped dead while we had our tongues in each other's mouths. And I don't know why he died. No one does. It doesn't look like we'll ever know what killed Dan.

And that means that I might as well go into a nunnery. Because after what happened with Dan, how can I even think about kissing a boy ever again?

What if the next boy I kiss drops dead, too?

Aunt Gwen's out today, thank God. I go in the back door and up the stairs to my room. I don't go over my schoolwork, of course. I take out the file, the special one, sit down on the floor, and spread all the clippings out around me. I do this when I'm feeling upset, or lonely, or depressed. So, guess what? I do this a lot.

It's as if I'm looking for clues, even though I know I won't find any.

BOY, 18, DIES IN FREAK ACCIDENT

I turn the clippings over one by one. I don't need to read them; I know them by heart. But somehow looking through them gives me a sense of calm, reminds me why I have this aching sense of emptiness and desperation lurking deep down inside me.

It's not even that Dan died in my arms, terrible as that was. It's that no one believed me when I tried to tell them I had no idea in the world what happened to him. Not the coroner at the inquest, not the police, not even, I think, my grandmother. No one.

And I sort of understand why. After all the lab tests came back inconclusive (they even went as far as testing my lipstick), the investigators were completely out of ideas. How in earth *could* Dan have died? The conclusion every-one seemed to jump to was the only one left: he somehow died from kissing me. It's ludicrous, I know. But we don't live in a world that deals well with the unexplained.

BAFFLING DEATH: KISS OF DEATH GIRL QUESTIONED

KISS OF DEATH GIRL: I WON'T CHANGE MY STORY

Yes, I got a nickname, like a serial killer they haven't caught yet. Like the Yorkshire Ripper or Son of Sam. And I should be grateful, because the reason they gave me a nickname is that I'm not eighteen yet. I'm still a minor, and you can't put a minor's name in the newspapers if they're connected with a crime, unless they're guilty.

Or dead.

They could print Dan's name all right. No problem there.

FOOD ALLERGY THE LIKELY CAUSE OF DAN MCANDREW'S TRAGIC DEATH

That's part of the mystery. The only thing the autopsy did show was that Dan had died of some type of extreme anaphylactic shock. Which means an allergic reaction. Dan was dangerously allergic to a variety of foods, including nuts, shellfish, and strawberries, but he didn't like talking about it with people. He was embarrassed by it and saw it as a weakness, his mother explained tearily during her testimony. Even though I cried the entire time, I was also trying to remember if I had eaten any of those things. But there was nothing to confess. I hadn't eaten anything that day which was on the list of toxic foods for Dan . . .

So that could only mean one thing. I'm the poison that killed him.

This is the other part of the mystery: Where was his EpiPen? His mum and dad swore blind at the inquest that he would never have gone anywhere without it. So how could he have forgotten it on the night of the party?

I wish there was a way to ask him. I wish there was a way to see and touch him. And although I dreamed for so long of kissing Dan's perfect lips, I wish above all that I never had.

eight

PLASTIC SURGERY-FREE ZONE

One of the very few bright spots in all of this is that I can set my alarm for eight-twenty and still be at school on time. It's a bare five-minute walk across the back lawn to the main house—or, as it is now, my school.

I pull on my favorite jeans and a purple sweater with green trim that Grandma got me for Christmas. (The colors sound awful together, but honestly, it looks nice. The green trim is really narrow. Grandma's good at clothes presents. And it's cashmere. Yummy.) I twist my hair up and fasten it at the back of my head with a silver clip, long and slender and pointed at one end, like a dagger. I've had this for years, but haven't worn it for a while, because at St. Tabby's, long hair clips have been *out* for the last six months. Elaborate big round tortoiseshell clasps, worn over buns at the nape of the neck, are *in*.

Count your blessings and all that. It's a ray of sunshine: at Wakefield Hall Girls' School, nobody cares about what they wear. There are no fashion police walking the corridors to laugh, point, and ridicule you because you're wearing a hair clip, which means you're *out*. It's super-intellectual here and, like I said, you have to wear the ghastly brown school uniform till you're sixteen anyway, so there's much less opportunity for fashion terrorism. The girls barely wear makeup, for God's sake. Phew. Much more relaxing.

I grab my old leather satchel and run downstairs just as Aunt Gwen starts to call my name. She's about to leave for school, too. (She's a teacher at Wakefield Hall—geography and Maths. See how awful my life is.) I wave a breakfast bar at her as she begins to spout off about growing girls needing to sit down to a proper meal in the morning, and dash out of the house, her grating metallic tones following me out the door. It's ten to nine as I pause outside the entrance to the old part of the school, which only the sixth-formers are allowed to use.

It's strange. I'm almost excited to be here.

Girls are flooding up the drive, the younger ones in their brown uniforms flowing past like a river of mud and through their own entrance in the nasty new modern building, glancing curiously at the older girls in normal clothes as they pass. I scarf down my breakfast bar and look around me at the girls my age. They're so dowdy by comparison to what I'm used to. Wakefield Hall is the anti–St. Tabby's. It's where parents send their daughters to get the best intellectual education money can buy, but, just as importantly, to be isolated in the countryside, free from the temptations of the big city (no fashion crazes, boys, drink, or drugs here). In a way, I'm grateful for that right now. The last thing I need is St. Tabby's, Part Two: The Revenge. Two years of boring dowdiness is just what I need to recover.

Nobody fashionable. Nobody wild. And no boys at all (well, apart from that gardener boy, but I'm just going to ignore him completely, so he doesn't count). Which is good, because I don't want to kill anyone else.

Oh, *Dan* . . . I see him lying on the terrace, the swiveling light of the ambulance below casting those eerie blue flashes over his body, I see them easing him onto a stretcher and covering him with a blanket, and I have to dig my fingernails into my palms to stop myself breaking down. The pain brings me back to the here and now. There are nasty red half-moons on my palms, but that's okay. As long as I didn't cry in public.

I look around and realize that, while I've been lost in miserable memories, everyone else has already gone up the steps. We're due in our classrooms any minute. No problem. I've been exploring this school building since I was tiny. I know it like the palm of my hand. I sling my satchel over my shoulder and dash inside and up the stairs, heading for Lower Six C. Right at the top, down the corridor, first right—

No! It's all changed! Lower Six C is now some sort of science lab! Grandmother—sorry, *Lady Wakefield*—has been doing massive remodeling without even mentioning it to me! And now there's no one around to ask for directions, because I'm so late that everyone's in their classrooms already, and I'm going to be there well past nine on my first day of school . . . . oh *bugger*. . . .

I arrive, panting and doubtless red-faced, at the new and, by the looks of it, not-much-improved Lower Six C, to find everyone already there but me: girls sitting in massed ranks at their desks, teacher looming in front of hers. Horrors. The whole room turns to stare as I stand in the doorway, and I know every girl there is thinking devoutly: "I'm *so glad* that isn't me."

I don't know the teacher in charge, but she's glaring at me as if I were something nasty she just stepped in.

"Scarlett Wakefield, I presume," she says nastily. "Since you probably haven't bothered to inform yourself of my name, I am Miss Newman."

No one is labeled a Ms. here. Grandmother—*Lady Wakefield*—is very old-fashioned.

"Yes," I blurt out. "I'm so sorry I'm late. I—"

"Oh, no need to explain, Scarlett. No need at all. We all assumed that you thought you could waltz into class any time you felt like it."

"No, honestly, I—"

"But let me tell you, Miss Wakefield, that just because your grandmother is the headmistress here, and your aunt the head of geography, I will not allow you any special privileges in my class. Your grandmother and aunt have issued strict edicts to that effect."

As Miss Newman is yelling at me, I somehow manage to notice that there's a clear mustache shadow above her upper lip. I think I can see a nose hair or two as well. She probably has hairy knuckles. And I don't even want to *think* about what her back's like.

"I was going to do you the courtesy of taking you aside and making this little point to you," she continues after a deep breath. "But since you have failed to show me and your fellow students the courtesy of showing up to class on time, I think I should respond in kind. I see that you are the type of girl to think that she can get away with anything she wants to because she has some sort of *special status*. Well, believe me, Miss Wakefield, that will not be the case *at all* for you. Your grandmother wished you to transfer to Wakefield Hall in the sixth form to have the advantages of our superb educational system for your A Levels, not because you were to be in any way *pampered* while you were here."

That's the official story—that I'm back here because Wakefield Hall is second to none in its record of girls getting top marks in their exams. No mention of my being effectively expelled from St. Tabby's for killing a boy. Grandmother thought that would put a bit of a damper on my ability to make friends. Goodness knows why.

"You may find a desk and take your seat in the few minutes we have remaining before leaving for assembly," Miss Newman says, her voice icy enough to freeze hot soup.

I've been ducking my head to avoid her awful sneer. I manage to lift my head and look around me frantically for a spare desk. Oh God. The only one left is in the second row, of course. I'm sitting with the keen, swotty girls. Great.

I do the Walk of Shame across the room and slip behind the desk, the last one in the row, next to the window Grandma's kept the old wooden desks from when she first started the school: they're ancient and battered, scarred by girls incising them with the nibs of fountain pens that they would fill from the built-in inkwells at the back. You can tell they were inkwells because they're stained from decades of leaks. Now they're just used for standing ballpoints in. I lift the lid of my desk and slide in my books. That's all that gets left in the desks: there are lockers downstairs now, with combination locks, for serious stuff. You can't have just wooden desks that anyone could open anymore, not when girls have iPods and cell phones and all kinds of expensive stuff that's highly nickable.

I look around. Hardly anyone meets my gaze. Great. They all hate me already. Miss Newman has managed to make everyone think I'm trying to take the piss and get away with murder because I'm the headmistress's grand-daughter. God, I hate my life.

There's one girl who does look back at me, though, and I'm immediately curious about her. She's tall, with wide shoulders and well-built upper arms. (I'm not being weird, but I notice these things because of gymnastics, okay?) Her hair is short, dark, and shaggy, falling round her face in an artfully clipped style that makes me think she's carefully arranged every lock, pieced it with wax or something, to seem so trendily disarranged. Her eyes are wide set, long, and green, and the look she's giving me is absolutely unreadable. I've got no bloody idea what she thinks of me at all.

The nine o'clock bell goes, and we all stand up and prepare to file into the Assembly Hall so Grandmother—*Lady Wakefield*—can lecture us all about Wakefield Hall's core values, and why good character is the most important possession a woman can boast, and all that Edwardian Young Ladies' Manual stuff she loves so much. And still none of the other girls are making any effort to include me in their tiny circles. I wasn't expecting to make a best friend on the first day, but this is definitely the worst-case scenario.

Stupid me. I should never say things like that. Because when the worst-case scenario really does turn up, I'll be left longing for the time when twenty girls in Lower Sixth C put their noses in the air and wouldn't look at me, and the twenty-first, having given me a long look, seemed to have decided that it wasn't worth her while even to make a point of ignoring me on principle. She's wearing a navy wool sweater with pieces of leather on the elbows, the kind of thing you only see on fishermen or someone's granddad. It's very old, I can see how frayed the cuffs are. Her combat trousers look equally ancient, like someone might actually have worn them into combat. They're clean—she'd never get away with wearing something stained at Wakefield Hall—but they're definitely screaming "hand-me-downs."

I look at the line of girls in front of me, and despite the noses in the air, I do see one reason to be cheerful: none of the aforesaid noses are bobbed or filed-down or artificially sculpted. As well as being fashion-, boy-, drink-, and drug-free, Wakefield Hall is equally a plastic surgery–free zone. It's such a world away from St. Tabby's that I really doubt anyone here has any connections to the London, *Teen Vogue*, shiny happy people scene, which means they're very unlikely to know that Scarlett Wakefield is known to the tabloid press by a much more lurid nickname.

If I'm lucky, I'll manage to keep my secret. Girls won't be keen to make friends with the headmistress's granddaughter. But befriending the Kiss of Death girl? That would be a whole different story.

nine

SHOWING OFF

"Meena, nicely done on the whole."

Mrs. Fisher, our Latin teacher, is passing between the desks, handing out our marked translation homework.

Meena, a stringy girl with droopy posture, looks very downcast at this verdict. I've noticed this already in my first few days at Wakefield Hall—the girls set incredibly high standards for themselves. I thought St. Tabby's was competitive, but this is way beyond anything that went on at St. Tabby's.

"Natalie!" Mrs. Fisher's brows contract severely as she stops in front of Natalie's desk. "We're in the sixth form now; we know the difference between the ablative and the dative case, surely?"

Natalie starts nodding so convulsively she looks defective, like a toy they'll have to recall before the head comes off.

"Well, *show* me next time!"

Mrs. Fisher drops the paper on Natalie's desk rather than handing it to her. Oh dear.

"Susan! *Lovely* use of the iambic pentameter! Top marks!"

Susan, a pretty girl with very pale skin, blushes so hard her entire face floods with red color, like blood poured into milk. She takes her paper back from Mrs. Fisher with a huge smile.

"Scarlett—" Mrs. Fisher turns to me.

I smile in anticipation. I've always been pretty good at Latin.

"A *lot* more work is going to be needed here, I'm afraid," Mrs. Fisher says. She doesn't drop the paper on my desk: she stands there, holding it, a horrible indication that there is more criticism to come.

"*Very* sketchy work. We're really going to have to concentrate on your written Latin. I can see that this has *not* been a priority for you."

I wait for the paper to fall on my desk so this public humiliation can finally be over, but she still doesn't let it go. Eventually I realize that she's waiting for an answer.

"Um, no," I manage. "We didn't have to do any written Latin for the GCSE exam, so . . . um . . ."

Mrs. Fisher sniffs.

"So your teacher didn't bother drilling you in it? *Very* short-sighted! And now we have to pick up her pieces, don't we?"

I nod humbly.

Finally she drops the paper on my desk.

"See me after class, Scarlett," she says. "We might want to downgrade your choice of Latin to an AS Level. That'll be much easier for you. I'm afraid that our choice of exam board is *rather* more rigorous than the one you've been used to."

I stagger out of Latin class a bleeding, broken girl. My pride is in tatters. I have been torn and shredded in front of an entire group of girls to whom translating Shakespeare into Latin iambic pentameter is what they do for a light intellectual warm-up before breakfast. Mrs. Fisher clearly thinks I should drop Latin. She as good as told me so. Bloody hell, *I* think I should drop Latin. I had no idea it was going to be this hard.

But now I have an awful feeling that I've been so humiliated that I have to stick with Latin, just to prove that I can do it. My pride won't let me drop it, even though in class just now I couldn't answer one question right. I was so demoralized I couldn't have managed a sentence as simple as "Sextus has six slaves and Decimus has a big dog."

I check my timetable. Oh, thank God. It's the last period of the morning, and Lower Sixth C has PE. Wakefield Hall is so old-school that they still call it physical education and make it compulsory till you're eighteen—at St. Tabby's it was gym, and you could drop it at fourteen in favor of just starving yourself to fit into size XS instead. Great, some exercise to take the edge off. I'm all wound up from being made to look a fool in front of eight Latin swots.

The changing rooms smell, as always, of feet and armpits. Eeww. I wind my hair into a tight ponytail, pull on the regulation white T-shirt and brown gym shorts, and jog into the gym. Wakefield Hall doesn't have anything like what we had at St. Tabby's, our huge gymnasium with its spring-loaded floors and its long tumble track. This is as big, but the floors are wood—*much* less bounce—no bars, no beams, let alone a tumble pit, and the trampoline isn't even set up all the time.

The girls are all filing in, looking, for the most part, extremely dispirited at having to be here—apart from the hockey/lacrosse contingent, a bunch of hard-edged tough chicks with thighs the size of hams and faces pink and weather-beaten from being outdoors in all weathers, trying to kill each other with big sticks of wood. Still, they don't intimidate me. I know they haven't trained as hard as I have for the past nine years.

I know I sound obnoxious. But honestly, these last few days at Wakefield Hall have been pretty rough. Latin was just the worst of a long series of classes that made me realize not only that I have a long way to go to catch up to Wakefield Hall's academic standards, but that I'm in for a really bad time from my teachers, because they're bending over backward not to show me any favoritism.

So it's understandable, isn't it, that I'm jumping with joy at finally getting to show off a bit at something I actually *know* I'm going to be better at than anyone here?

"Lower Sixth! Hello!" says a bright, metallic voice. "I am Miss Carter! And we're all here to get fit and learn good habits that will *keep* us fit for the rest of our lives, aren't we?"

"Yes, Miss Carter," the girls chorus dully, staring miserably at their shoes.

This is *not* a sporty school.

"So let's start with a nice warm-up, shall we? Get the blood flowing!"

Miss Carter is one of those jolly-hockey-stick types. She looks like one of the field-sport girls, all grown up and happily settled down with another ex-field-sport girl in a cozy little cottage on the school grounds. Her hair is short and blond, her skin looks like it's never seen a makeup wand, and her thighs and arms are as pink and hamlike as those of the hockey/lacrosse toughs. She makes us do jumping jacks and knee-ups in series. It's unintentionally hilarious. There are more bosoms bouncing around in the gym than in an R&B music video. These girls are totally not wearing decent sports bras. (I worked out my problem over the summer, by the way. You get a minimizer bra from Marks and Spencer's and wear a pull-on sports bra over that. Two layers. Squash 'em down.)

Still, there's a lovely view outside. The outer wall of the gym has floor-to-ceiling glass windows that look out onto a wide stretch of rich green grassy sports fields—hockey on one side, lacrosse on the other, separated from each other by Lime Walk, a long avenue of lime trees raised up slightly with a gentle green hill sloping down on either side of the avenue and smoothing off into the sports fields. The trees are rich with autumn leaves, the grass is green and thick. In a couple of months' time, the sports fields will be muddy and churned-up from being pounded by cleats on the bottom of the tough girls' shoes, but right now it's a beautiful autumn landscape, with the leaves just starting to turn golden.

Miss Carter blows a whistle, and the girls stop jumping and jog over to the trampoline. Honestly, she reminds me of a dog trainer. Any minute now she'll make us all sit up and beg for treats.

"Sharon Persaud! You're up first!" she yells enthusiastically.

Sharon Persaud clambers grimly onto the trampoline, looking very hostile. Being of Asian origin, Sharon is not as weather-beaten as the white sporty girls, but that she's one of them is all too clear from the heft of her muscular thighs and bulging calves.

"She scares me *so much*," whispers a girl next to me.

I've noticed this girl before; she stands out at Wakefield Hall because of her discreet, expensively highlighted hair, a mouse-brown lightened to a subtle caramel. It wouldn't be anything out of the ordinary at St. Tabby's, but here it's pretty unusual. She's also wearing makeup—mascara and eye pencil—which she needs, because her eyes are very small and deep-set, and they have a perpetually nervous expression, which is intensified as Sharon starts jumping dourly up and down on the tramp. With every landing, the tramp thuds as Sharon's large, trainer-shod feet plonk down. She's not jumping high, just heavily.

"She's taken out two girls' front teeth with her hockey stick," whispers Nervous Girl. "They had to get implants."

"*Christ.*"

"I'm so happy hockey isn't compulsory anymore," says Nervous Girl. "I used to jump away every time I saw her charging down the field with that lavender hockey stick. I had to wear braces for a *year*, just for my overbite. I couldn't go through that again."

"Lizzie, no talking there!" Miss Carter sings out. "Good work, Sharon! Now, who's next?"

She hasn't taken her eyes off me, so I know what's coming.

"New girl! It's Scarlett, isn't it? You're a bit of a gymnast, aren't you? Off you go, then!"

"Can I take my trainers off?" I ask.

"No, rules are rules for everyone," Miss Carter says, but her tone is perfectly pleasant, no snottiness, which is a welcome change for a Wakefield Hall teacher.

Sharon jumps down from the trampoline, the wooden floor creaking in protest as she lands. I vault up instead, and though it's ridiculous, my heart is pounding with excitement. I haven't been on a tramp for three months. I am so out of shape. But it's wonderful to be back, even on a soggy tramp with a whole group of girls standing round the sides to gawk at me.

I do a few bounces, to get a feel of the tramp. Then I take off. Jump, set, front tuck, land, three front somersaults in a row. The girls are ooh-ing and aah-ing, but I tune it out. If at first this was about showing off—showing the whole of Lower Sixth C that yes, Scarlett Wakefield is actually good at *something*, believe it or not—as soon as I started jumping, that impulse faded. Because the sheer joy of being on a tramp again, working on my skills, has flooded through me like the best kind of drug you could possibly imagine, the kind your own body makes all by itself, and I'm high—literally and metaphorically. Ha ha. I'm flipping myself like a pancake. God, I forgot how much I loved tramp, the height it gives you, the extra bounce that allows you to spin and twist through the air.

Jump, set, knees to chest and right over myself in a tight little ball, open up and land, back tuck. One, two, three. I'm a bit dizzy, but I can't stop. Front pike, front layout. Easy stuff, but I don't have traveling room on this tramp, the springs are all exposed and they scare me, particularly in trainers. Ricky, my old coach, blew out his knee doing demonstration jumps on a trampoline in trainers. He turned the flange on one of his shoes under him in a bad landing. With bare feet, it would just have been an ankle sprain, but because of the shoes, his whole foot turned under him and his knee popped with the torque. He had to have a ton of surgery, and his knee's never been right since. The scars track each side of his knee, wobbly white lines, and the knee itself is oddly shaped, as if you were looking at it through pebble glass.

Ricky's knee has always been a big symbol, because Ricky messed it up showing off, knowing that he should be more careful because he was in trainers. So now I rein myself in. No twists. *Don't get cocky! That's how you get hurt!* I can hear Ricky's voice in my head, and suddenly I miss him and gymnastics so much I have to catch my breath.

I don't go for anything too ambitious. No back hand-springs, I'll travel too far. I finish with a back step-out layout, and it goes so well I blast off into another. It's old-fashioned, we don't do it in competition, but I've always enjoyed it. You land on one leg and then the other follows, like spokes of a wheel turning under you. It looks dazzlingly pretty.

Everyone's clapping. I shake my head back, embarrassed, but I can't deny the thrill. My back feels looser, pulled out by the stretch of the back layouts.

"I don't suppose anyone wants to follow that, do they?" Miss Carter says, grinning. "Any volunteers feeling brave? No? Then it's time for circuit training!"

Groans arise. Miss Carter has set up an entire circuit in the back part of the gym, and she briskly indicates what each station is for. It's *really* old-school—no music, just the sound of girls panting and groaning next to me, inter-spersed with Miss Carter yelling things like "Come *on*, Lizzie!" and blowing her whistle to indicate that we need to change station.

"Anyone who wants to push herself," Miss Carter calls, "can finish up with some optional leg lifts on the bars!"

I'm across the gym in a flash. The suckers for punishment are me, three hockey/lacrosse tough nuts (they never smile, those girls, I bet they're so busy practicing their intimidating faces they don't even smile in their sleep), and the big-shouldered, shaggy-haired girl who has the desk next to me. Wow. Her thighs are bulging out of the brown gym shorts: her quads must be really strong. I look down at my own. Much slimmer, but God, her calves are so cut. I wouldn't want to be that big (I remember Dan commenting on how small I was and how feminine that made me feel) but I can't help envying her strength, so obviously on display.

"Good, two keen new girls!" Miss Carter says. "Taylor, isn't it?"

Big Shoulders nods. She's not a chatty one, I've noticed that already in class.

"Right, up you all go. The rest of you, stretch it out, please."

We climb up the monkey bars, swivel our hands to grasp under the top bar, and hang in place, waiting for the whistle. When it comes, we grip for dear life and start lifting our feet to our heads—ideally. Out of the corner of my eye, I can see the hockey girls barely managing to lift to waist height. They're strong, all right, but that's a lot of weight to lift, and they don't do the ab work gymnasts do. And all that bending over the hockey stick must give them really tight backs. But Taylor is pumping away next to me, her big strong legs shooting up as if she does this all day, every day.

I'm shocked. And I'm pissed off. I realize how much I've been expecting to be the best at PE, how much it mattered to me, at this school where I feel like I'm the worst at every single academic subject I'm taking. It comes over me like an angry wave, and I see bright angry competitive red, and I curl my back and tuck my abs and haul away at lifting my legs with everything I've got, and still that Taylor girl is going higher and faster and more effortlessly than I am.

She knows we're competing. I can tell. And when the whistle goes, the two of us don't stop. The hockey girls have long climbed down, but Taylor and I keep going, though my feet are only at waist height now, while Taylor's still doing high lifts, she seems to be on some sort of girl steroids, or maybe she's an android, while I, frankly, am absolutely knackered.

The whistle's going again.

"Girls! Time to stop!" Miss Carter is bellowing.

Thank God. I flail for a low bar with my feet, find it, and climb down. My palms are burning, accustomed as I am to a padded bar, not just bare wood. Taylor drops to the floor next to me, and I notice how light her landing is, despite her big muscular body.

I glance at her resentfully. Our eyes meet. It's a stand-off. Hers are narrowed, long, and seemingly even greener against the paleness of her skin, outlined by unexpectedly thick dark lashes. For a moment I think Taylor's going to say something. And then she turns away, deliberately snubbing me.

Cow. I hate her. The only girl I've got something in common with here—she's a new girl, too—and she turns out to be a snotty cow who can beat me at leg lifts.

I hate this godforsaken armpit of a school in the middle of nowhere. I hate the teachers who make me feel like an uneducated moron.

And most of all, I hate this Taylor girl. She'd better stay well away from me from now on.

Ten

"WHO PUSHED ME?"

When I was little, my nanny read me that story about the man who knew the king had ears like a donkey. He had to swear on his life not to tell anyone. But after a while, he couldn't bear it—the secret was too big for him to keep. So he went down to the river and whispered into the rushes: "The king has donkey's ears! The king has donkey's ears!"

And then someone wove a basket out of those rushes, and the basket told everyone the king had donkey's ears. Or something. I'm not really sure about the end of it. And I don't remember, either, why the king had donkey's ears in the first place. Some fairy probably cursed him. That's how weird things always happen in these kinds of stories, isn't it?

Anyway, I didn't understand the point of the story when I was small. I was caught up in wondering what it would be like to have donkey's ears. I mean, they'd be all big and itchy, and how would you hide them? Even under a big hat, it would be pretty difficult. But my nanny said that the story was a fable, which means it's meant to teach you a lesson, and the lesson was that it's really hard to keep a secret.

I didn't get that, either. I mean, everyone already knows it's hard to keep a secret, don't they?

I asked my mother, but she just looked at me blankly and waved me away and went on talking to whoever was on the end of the phone. I was too young then to realize there wasn't much point asking my mother anything important.

But now I understand it was my nanny who got it wrong. The lesson is not that it's hard to keep a secret.

The lesson is that it's impossible to keep a secret.

This is too much for me to hold. I feel as if I'm going to explode with it. My head actually hurts with the effort of not telling anyone what I saw.

I can't ring anyone—the police especially—and tell them anonymously. They can trace any call; they can record anything and prove it's your voice. It's the same with e-mails. Everyone knows you don't have any privacy with e-mails. And handwriting. And computer printers. I'm sure I saw a TV show about that. And right now, I'm so scared that I don't want to take any risks. Or because there's always some risk, let's face it. I want to take the least amount of *risks possible. The least amount of stuff that could lead back to me.*

Because I have to tell. I have to pass this on. And once I've told, I'll be free. Won't I? I'll be free, because it'll be someone else's responsibility. I'll have passed it on to the person who needs to hear it. The person who got blamed for it.

And hopefully, once I've told, whenever I close my eyes I'll stop seeing that moment, the moment I can't stop remembering. The moment at the party when I saw what I wasn't supposed to see.

. . .

There are three e-mails in my in-box, if you don't count the spam. And these three definitely aren't spam. They're meant specifically for me.

I know that because although I don't recognize any of the senders' names, when the subject line says stuff like *Killed anyone else yet?* Or *You bloody bitch I hope you die!* It's pretty obvious that they're coming from Plum and about twenty or so girls who, if Plum told them to eat dirt, would get down there with their faces in the ground and start chewing. You've got to admire her leadership skills. She'd be great in the army.

I closed all my e-mail accounts and opened new ones with names no one would think would be me. I changed my mobile phone number. But at Wakefield Hall, I get an e-mail account automatically, and it wouldn't take a master spy to work out that anything sent to scarlettwakefield@wakefieldhall.edu would probably reach me. None of them are coming from addresses I recognize, but that doesn't mean anything.

I know they're coming from girls at St. Tabby's.

I shiver, remembering the last time I was there, when they sent me to clear out my locker on my own. No teacher with me. And after the headmistress had made me go into her office to listen to a lecture about bringing the school into disrepute, I was too proud to plead for an escort.

Stupid, stupid. That pride thing gets me every time.

They were waiting for me, of course. Plum, Nadia, Venetia, Chloe, and at least ten others. Captain Plum had rallied her troops. Designer uniforms by Prada and Stella McCartney. The stacked platform heels would make it hard to run, but they didn't need to. Just circle me, and kick me when I was down.

I stare at the hateful e-mails in my in-box and click on them, one by one, to delete them without reading the content. It'll just be pictures of me, with "Killer Slut" written over them. Or articles about murdered girls, with "Maybe she stole someone else's boyfriend" on the subject line.

Whatever they send me, at least it's not as bad as having them all back me against my locker and shout insults at me. Apart from Dan's death, that's the memory I most want to erase forever.

But I can't. I remember it so clearly it might as well be happening right now.

• • •

"Oh look. It's the school murderess," Plum began, in that tone of fake surprise that princesses perfect in the cradle. "Who're you going to kill today, Scarlett?"

Several tart responses sprang to my lips, but I knew that uttering any snappy retorts would be roughly equivalent to lying down on the ground and inviting everyone to jump on me. This was going to be bad enough without me chucking any fuel on the fire. I kept my head ducked and inserted my key into the door of my locker.

"Oh, she's got ages yet, Plum," Venetia chimed in. "It's only noon. She's got twelve hours to go before she kills someone else's boyfriend!"

I was rummaging through my locker, trying to block out their voices. I thought I could imagine everything they were going to throw at me, and I'd played it through in my head beforehand, trying to brace myself. But that I didn't expect, and my head jerked back, bumping into the locker door, much to my annoyance.

Plum was delighted to have got a response from me.

"Yes, that's right, bitch," she hissed. "You stuck your tongue down my boyfriend's throat and you killed him."

"She's a slut," chimed in none other than Sophia Von und Zu Unpronounceable. Despite her being Austrian, she had an

English nanny and governess, apparently, and her accent was spot-on: you'd never know she was foreign. I had to admire her effortless command of current British slang as she continued fluently: "A stupid, dirty little boyfriend-stealing slut!"

I was gobsmacked. I couldn't believe that Plum was actually claiming that Dan was her boyfriend. My brain was frantically scrolling back through the brief time I saw them together, and nothing about their behavior remotely suggested to me any relationship between them. It was Dan who came after me. Well, of course it was! How would I have the nerve to pursue a boy as hot as Dan McAndrew? But if I'd had the faintest idea that he and Plum were together, I would never have gone out onto the terrace with him.

Partly that was self-protection. If I'd accepted an invitation like that from Plum's boyfriend, I might as well have chucked myself off the terrace directly afterward. But mostly, it was pride, yet again. I wouldn't want a boy who belonged to someone else. I wouldn't want to share. If I ever kissed another boy, I wanted to feel that 100% of his attention was on me. That I was the only one he wanted.

I couldn't help it, even though I knew I was digging an even deeper hole for myself. I pulled back from my locker, looked Plum right in the eye and said sarcastically, "Right. You're really claiming Dan was your boyfriend?"

There was a split second of silence. Sophia, who was standing next to Plum, darted her eyes sideways to see Plum's reaction to my challenge, and I knew in that moment that I was right. Dan and Plum weren't a couple.

It didn't help me, though. Far from it.

"You stupid little bitch!" *Plum hissed. "As if you knew any-*thing *about me and Dan! You were only invited to Nadia's party because Simon wanted to get off with you. I bet you actually thought we'd asked you because we thought you were cool." She razored me with an up-and-down stare that felt as if I was being sliced to ribbons. "What, did you think we wanted to get* fashion *tips from you?"*

Everyone laughed sycophantically at this witticism.

"Simon thought you'd be an easy shag," Plum continued cruelly, her eyes still so slitted-up with rage that I could barely see the irises, "and he was right, wasn't he? Because you hadn't been there longer than ten minutes before you got my boyfriend to snog you and you bloody killed *him, you nasty poisoning* little tart!"

I was completely humiliated. I thought about all the trouble I took to buy clothes, to do my makeup, to try to fit in, and all the time no one had any intention of being friends with me. I was just a present for Simon.

I was about to burst into tears, and if I did, I would have had to kill myself. Nothing would be worse than breaking down in front of Plum Saybourne and her circle of mocking faces. Thank God, a bell went, and the surprise of it enabled me to take a long deep swallow, camouflaged by the sound, and squeeze the tears back down into their ducts again.

Plum was momentarily interrupted by the noise—we were in the basement, and the bell really resonated down there, it felt as if the walls were vibrating. I ducked into my locker again and sniffed a couple of times, just to be sure my nose wouldn't run and give me away. I'd given up caring about getting my stuff now—I just wanted to get out of there as fast as possible. But I grabbed some things at random and shoved them into my satchel, so it looked as if they hadn't managed to distract me from doing what I came here to do.

This clearly infuriated Plum. I felt a push on my back, and I stumbled, off-balance because I was holding the satchel, and only just managed not to hit my head again on the side of the locker.

It made my brain tighten, like a fist closing on itself. I took a deep breath. I grabbed everything from my locker that I could conceivably want or need and I filled up my satchel. Then I slammed the door shut, slinging the satchel over my shoulder, and turned with my back to the lockers, and said in a quiet voice that even I could hear was menacing, "Who pushed me?"

And I looked at each girl in turn. They were all prettily made-up. Their hair was shiny and smooth, their eyes opened wide with mascara, their skin medicated to be acne-free, their legs waxed, their heels high.

And me? I was in jeans and a T-shirt, my hair pulled back into a messy ponytail. No makeup. Boring old trainers. And I bet none of them could do a single full-body push-up. I was so much stronger than them. It flashed into my brain that I was longing for a fight. It was an awful, primitive impulse, and it shocked me worse than that push in my back.

"WHO PUSHED ME?" I said, louder now, and I fixed each of them with a hard-core stare. Some of them shuffled their

feet: some of them took a step back. Sophia's saggy rag-doll pos-
ture crumpled as if someone just hung her off a peg.

I had to say something for Plum: she wasn't a coward. She
was the only girl who wasn't intimidated by me.

"I did," she said, tossing her mane of chestnut hair. "You de-
served it. Slut. You're only here to pick up your things because
you're being expelled, *so just get them and go, because no one*
wants you here."

Every word was like a stab. I couldn't stand it anymore. I ad-
vanced on her, and I heard myself say:

"You shut up, or—"

"Or what?" Plum taunted, shoving her face forward. "Don't
think you can just sneak back to your grandma's poxy school for
brainiac nerds and hide out there like you hadn't killed someone!
Just because you didn't have your name in the papers, do you
really think all the girls there won't know exactly who you are
after I get through with you? We're going to make sure that
everyone at Wakefield Hall knows exactly who you are and
what you did!"

In her anger, she had stepped toward me, shouting her threats
right into my face. We were so close I could see how smooth her
skin was. I could smell her perfume. I could see the fury in her
eyes, matching my own.

And I put out my hands, caught her upper arms and
slammed her back against the locker behind her so hard that the
entire row of them rattled and shook. With glee, I saw the expres-
sion in her eyes switch from anger to fear as I held her there, my

127

fingers biting into her biceps, and she broke off midinsult, the next evil words she had been going to shout caught dead in her throat.

Plum Saybourne was scared of me. And she was right to be.

"If you even try to get in touch with any girl at Wakefield Hall," I said, dangerously quiet, "I will tell my grandmother what you did. And she will get you expelled from here."

"No she won't," Plum said, doing her best to toss her head, but failing, as it was trapped against the locker.

"Oh yes, she will," I contradicted. "I just had a long lecture upstairs about bringing St. Tabby's into disrepute. The last thing they want here is anymore scandal or talk about Dan. If they hear you're spreading it to other schools, they'll kick you out of here so fast and hard your bony arse will be sore for weeks. And don't think any other school will take you when they know the reason you got kicked out of St. Tabby's."

I'm not sure whether that last bit was true or not, but it still worked on Plum.

"You bitch," she hissed at me.

"Mirror mirror," I snapped back.

She tried to bring a hand up to hit me, but I easily held her, the muscles in my arms bunching only slightly with the effort. The grip of my hands, which could hold me as I did huge swings around the asymmetric bars, which could support my weight in a handstand walk, were much, much stronger than any muscle in Plum's skinny starved-to-a-size-XXS body. She was no physical match for me, and she knew it, and for once in her life, I had managed to cause a genuine, honest look of terror on Plum Saybourne's beautiful face.

I had no idea what I was going to do. But suddenly I was more scared of myself than the girl I was holding.

"Scarlett Wakefield!" called a teacher's voice from the stair landing. "Scarlett, are you still there?"

Her heels clattered down the stairs, and paused. As soon as I heard my name being called, I'd let Plum go and stepped back, but I was surrounded by a semicircle of girls who had moved forward to see what was happening between me and Plum. Plum had folded her arms across herself, and was rubbing her biceps with her hands, wincing theatrically.

"I hope there isn't a problem here, girls?" the teacher said, in a voice that indicated that there had better not be.

"No, Ms. Moore," Plum said demurely. Butter wouldn't melt in her mouth. "We were just saying good-bye to Scarlett."

"I'm glad to hear it," Ms. Moore said drily. "Scarlett, your grandmother is waiting."

I gave Plum a last threatening look, and though she was no Sophia—I couldn't make her go floppy—at least she flinched. A small victory for me. I turned on my heel and the group of girls shifted quickly, making room for me to pass through them.

"Scarlett?" Plum called.

I shouldn't have looked back. But I did.

"Best of luck the next time you kiss someone!" she said, widening her eyes, which made her look so beautiful that the contrast of her pretty face and her poisonous words was really creepy.

"Plum!" said Ms. Moore sharply, but the damage was done. Plum had won. Twice over. She'd won because she pushed

129

me so far I'd actually used my grandmother to threaten her, something I hated myself for having done.

And she'd won because, with her unerring instinct for people's weak spots, she had identified mine and driven a sharp knife right into it. When the inquest couldn't identify what had killed Dan—beyond saying that he had died of an allergic reaction, of course—it was like they had given me a life sentence, even though I hadn't been accused of anything. Until I knew what had killed Dan, how could I ever kiss a boy again? I would be too terrified that he would drop dead at my feet.

Plum knew that, and she'd used it against me. I might have momentarily got the better of Plum Saybourne by scaring her witless, but she managed to get inside my head and single out my biggest fear.

God, I hated her.

eleven

MILLSTONES AND ROPE BURN

There's a ping as another e-mail comes in. I stare at the
sender, unable, for a moment, to believe what I'm seeing.
Then I grab my mouse and click on it, hoping against
hope . . .

From: gymgirlalison@pipserve.co.uk
To: scarlettwakefield@wakefieldhall.edu
Subject: [left blank]
Stop ringing me and Luce. We don't want to
talk to you. Plum and everyone are really
picking on us cuz we were friends of yours
which is COMPLETELY UNFAIR and it's doing
my head in. Don't reply to this. Luce says
the same but she is so cross with you she
wouldn't even write to you. Just pretend
that we don't exist, like that day you went
off with Plum and sat on her stupid fountain. We'll NEVER FORGIVE YOU.

I delete it so fast my fingers almost scorch the keys.

Sometimes I feel even guiltier about betraying Luce and Alison than I do about Dan's death, because I don't know how Dan died, or what I did to cause it. But Luce and Alison—I know for certain it was all my fault.

There's no one I can talk to about this. And because I can't talk about it, I feel as if I'll never be free of it. Dan is dead, and his death will hang around my neck forever. There's some expression like that, I think. Having a millstone round your neck, that's it. And what I did to Luce and Alison—turning my back on them, walking away from our friendship—is a millstone, too. My guilt is weighing me down, pressing on me so it feels hard to breathe.

I have to get out of the house. It's five-thirty. I was going to do some homework, but now my mood's so bad that I can't concentrate. I thunder down the stairs, taking them two at a time and raising a complaint from Aunt Gwen, who's in her office marking essays. I barely register her, though, because I'm thinking about millstones. They're big and round and they have a hole in the middle. I expect the idea came from that hole—you imagine having a big heavy stone slung over your head, hanging round your neck, so heavy that you could barely stand up under its weight, let alone walk or run. That's what my depression is like, a weight so backbreaking that it's a real struggle to act normally—worse, sometimes I don't think I even know what acting normally is.

I killed someone. Someone I really liked. It's not just

that Dan is dead, it's that my dreams of getting to know him, going out with him, maybe even falling in love with him, have been shattered. And I never kissed anyone before. It was the most amazing kiss, and it was over almost before it began. I'm scared I'll never have that again, an incredible physical connection with a boy. I've lost something that I only had for the briefest moment, but was the best thing that had ever happened to me in my life.

Oh yes, and I betrayed my two best friends just so I could go to a stupid party where I was supposed to be the going-home present for Simon, who didn't even know me.

No wonder there's an enormous great whacking mill-stone round my neck.

Thankfully, it's a nice autumn day outside. Golden leaves are falling slowly from the trees that line the drive, moving gently in the light breeze, like the snow in those paperweights that you shake up and watch settle again. The leaves almost seem to be in slow motion, a cloud of pale yellow, glinting in the sunlight, descending gradually, buoyed up by the wind currents, to settle on the glinting green grass. I put out my hand, seeing if I can catch a leaf for good luck, but nothing falls into my hand. What a surprise.

To my right are the official school grounds. I could go and wander round the lake, or get lost in the maze, or sit beneath the weeping willow trees and indulge my gloomy mood. But I don't feel like doing anything that clichéd. I want to explore, I want an adventure. I want to distract myself from my thoughts and my memories. And as I look over

toward the hedge that surrounds the rose garden, I see someone trimming it.

It's that gardener guy. As I watch him clipping away at
the top of the hedge, evening it out, he senses that I'm looking at him, and he raises his head. He's too far away for me
to really make out his features, but I think I can see white
teeth flash in a smile, and he lifts one hand from the heavy
secateurs to raise it in a wave to me.

No. No, no no. My fault for looking at him, for getting
his attention. Everything's my fault at the moment. I can't
deal with a boy, can't even talk to him. Look what happened
the last time I did that! Immediately, I turn my back and
walk away, crossing the drive, my trainers crunching on the
gravel. In a moment, I'm in the thick stand of trees on the
other side, hidden from his gaze.

Six feet in, there's a high wooden fence. Beyond the
fence are the real woods, the ones that separate Wakefield
Hall from the public park beyond. There's another, much
higher fence, made of wrought iron, that runs between the
woods and the park, making sure no intruders can come in.
But this fence isn't to keep out intruders, it's to stop the girls
from going into the woods. The school grounds, though
large and sprawling, are patrolled by teachers strolling
around, keeping an eye on what the girls are up to: but you
can't patrol woods. You could hide there for days if you
wanted. Which is why the woods are off-limits, and why
there's this high wooden fence running around them, just in
case some girls are naughty enough to disobey the extremely

strict rule set in stone by my grandmother—sorry, *Lady Wakefield* . . .

Still, if a girl is really determined, this fence isn't exactly Fort Knox standards. I mean, it doesn't have rolls of barbed wire round the top, or anything really daunting. I look around me, but there's no one on the drive—no girls coming back from the village, eating Snickers bars and gossiping, no Aunt Gwen deciding to follow me out and see what I'm up to. I walk along the fence for a minute, sizing it up. Then I reach up to an overhanging tree branch and test it, seeing if it'll take my weight. It doesn't even bend.

I get a good grip on it, holding on tight, and I swing myself up, walking up the fence, bracing the soles of my feet to take some of my weight, till my feet reach the top of the fence. My knees bend, and I walk my hands up along the branch till I'm squatting on the top of the fence and I can see the other side. I push off and jump down. It's an easy landing. One thing I'm used to is jumping. Ricky used to make us do squat jumps up and down onto solid foam blocks almost half our height for minutes on end, grabbing the back of our T-shirts to haul us up as we flagged, yelling in our ears to motivate us.

I miss Ricky, but I miss Luce and Alison more.

Ugh, that e-mail! The guilt is like something stabbing me right through one ear and coming out the other side. I push Luce and Alison out of my mind as best I can, because there's nothing I can do about them, and look around me. The wood is very quiet; as soon as I landed behind the wall,

135

it was if a heavy silence settled here, as if the falling leaves are muffling any noise that might reach me.

It's wonderful. Total peace. Why have I never come back here before? My brain races: I can spend most of my after-school time here if I want. As long as I show up for dinner at seven in the school dining room, no one will know or care where I am the rest of the time. Aunt Gwenn will be glad to have me out of the house. If she even bothers to wonder about my whereabouts, she'll probably just assume I'm in the library doing my homework. Not that she'll give a damn anyway.

A bird is chirping overhead, and I can hear the whir of wings as another one joins it. This is so calm. Complete solitude: just me and the birds. I lean back against the tree, surveying the woods, the blue sky above, visible here and there through the thick cover of the branches, which are still heavy with leaves. I think about coming here every afternoon, isolating myself completely from the world outside, and the idea is so very tempting that it makes me wonder how healthy it would actually be. If you're being pushed away by everyone, is it really best to let that happen? To hide behind a wall and let the leaves fall on your head?

And just as I'm debating this with myself, I see movement through the trees, and I hear what sounds like grunting. I jump: I thought I was completely alone here. There are squirrels scurrying through the branches, rustling the leaves, but the shape I can see is a lot bigger than a squirrel. And it's in the tree, about halfway up . . . wait, what kind of animal is that big? For a moment I'm really scared. Then I tell myself that this is England, and there are no large, dangerous animals in the trees. Pull yourself together, Scarlett. I mean, even a polecat or some kind of wild forest cat couldn't be that big . . . and a dog couldn't climb like that. . . .

Now my curiosity is kicking in. I creep closer, careful where I put my feet, so I don't snap any branches and alert whoever, or whatever, to my presence. I pick my way gradually over the forest floor of mulch, broken twigs, and brown ferny debris fallen from the trees. The shape in the trees is moving, descending now, and then I hear a panting gasp and a thud as it lands. I freak and duck behind a tree. That was definitely a person. No animal makes noises like that. But who on earth could be out here in this no-man's-land behind the fence, climbing trees?

I peer out from behind the tree and my jaw drops. I actually feel the muscles loosen. Lots of wild speculations were running through my mind, but this is way off any of them. It's the last thing I would have expected to see.

It's that girl Taylor, the big-shouldered, shaggy-haired one who does phenomenal leg lifts. And now I realize how Taylor got those big shoulders and that enviably muscular back. She's halfway up a rope, which she has somehow slung around a high tree branch and fastened securely, securely enough for her to be able to put her entire body weight on it as she climbs up it.

Wow. I've climbed rope myself in gymnastics, but we always did that climb where you wrap the rope round one foot and stand on it with the other, pushing down with your feet, so you're not taking your whole weight with your arms. Taylor isn't doing that. She's climbing like a man, hauling herself up with her arms alone. I can see the muscles in her arms and back straining and swelling with the effort. Her breath is coming in short quick spurts, and the sweat's dampening the back of her tank top.

Bloody hell. This is a really hard-core workout. Taylor reaches the tree branch above, and with one hand, slaps it, as if she's scoring. Then she grabs back for the rope with her free hand and starts descending the rope again, still only using her arms.

She's coming down too fast, I think. I got rope burns doing that once, and I wince, watching her; that's got to hurt a bit.

There's that noise again as she lands, thudding down with a grunt that signals release from major physical effort. She looks at her palms ruefully. I was right; she's given herself rope burn. And then she kneels down, picks up something, and swivels round, facing in my direction.

The rope burn can't be that bad. Because what she's holding is a big tree branch, gripping it tightly, double handed, as if she knows how to use it. She's holding it like some sort of bat, and frankly the sight is pretty scary.

Especially because she's starting to walk toward the tree I'm hiding behind.

"I know you're there!" she yells menacingly. "I know you're behind that tree! Come on, show yourself!"

Jesus. I duck back behind the tree. I could make a run for it, but then she'd chase me, and what if I tripped and fell and she whacked me with the branch? I peer out between some leaves. She's nearly on me, and her face is set and angry.

Five seconds. Four. Three. I've left it too late to run, and that would be cowardly anyway. She's almost at the tree. I jump out, hands in the air.

"It's okay!" I scream. It's humiliating to hear how panicky I sound. "It's Scarlett! Don't hit me!"

THE LARA CROFT OF TEENAGE GIRLS

We stare at each other for a long moment. God, Taylor looks scary holding that branch, with her muscles bulging. She's wearing a white tank top with the wide straps of a sports bra showing at her neck, and loose green combat trousers hanging off her hips. I can see a flash of an incredibly flat and muscular stomach showing between the T-shirt and the trousers. She looks like a Marine, or an action heroine— the Lara Croft of teenage girls. After what feels like hours, she lets the branch fall to the ground. I'm very relieved to hear it land.

"How did you know I was here?" I ask.

"I could see your T-shirt," she says. "Next time you come sneaking through the woods, wear something that blends in better than bright red, okay?"

"I wasn't sneaking," I say indignantly. "You were making a racket I could hear from miles away. No wonder I wanted to see what was going on."

"I wasn't *that* loud," Taylor says, but I have her on the defensive now.

"Yes, you were. You were grunting like a wild boar."

"I was *not*!" She's furious. Her eyes narrow. "So what are you doing here? I expect you've got a key to the gate, because you're, like, the granddaughter of the stately home, or something?"

"There's a gate?"

Taylor jerks her head back, indicating the far side of the woods. "Back there," she says. "Don't tell me you climbed the wall."

"Oh right," I say sarcastically, "like you're the only person who can climb anything, I suppose. At least I didn't give myself rope burn."

"I only got rope burn because I was coming down fast to see who was spying on me."

"I wasn't spying on you!"

"*Right.* That's why you walked right out into the open and said 'hello,' I guess."

"Oh, forget it." I'm angry too, because she's caught me. I suppose I *was* spying on her a bit. I turn on my heel to go.

"Wait a minute," Taylor says sharply. "You'd better not tell anyone about seeing me here."

If she'd just asked me nicely, or not said anything at all, just taken it for granted that I wouldn't tell on her . . . that would have been fine. But the threatening tone of her voice makes me want to kick her in the shins.

Instead I just walk away.

"Don't you dare tell anyone!" Taylor shouts after me. "I mean, it, Scarlett!"

"I'd cross my fingers if I were you!" I shout back.

Of course I'm not going to run to a teacher and tell her that Taylor's climbing a rope in the woods. What kind of suck-up does she think I am? But equally, I'm not going to reassure her if she's going to be that nasty and suspicious.

She can just sweat it out for a while, till she realizes I'm not going to tell. I hope it makes her really nervous.

Serves her right for being such a grumpy cow.

*   *   *

I look at the envelopes, lying on the bed next to me. One is bulging slightly. Well, it would. Two hundred and fifty pounds, in ten-pound notes, make a pretty big wodge of cash. And the other one . . . the other one is practically flat. Again, that makes sense. All it has inside is one folded sheet of paper.

I still haven't decided whether I'm going to do this or not.

I pick the two white envelopes up and slide them into a bigger one, a brown manila envelope, fiddling the metal tongue through the little hole, pushing it down to close the flap. And my brain slides off suddenly into one of its weird tangents, the way it does when I've been really good with my diet and I get a bit dizzy and feel like I'm floating a foot off whatever surface I'm supposedly on.

Why are they called "manila" envelopes? my brain is asking. Did they get invented in Manila? And where is Manila, anyway? Is it some town in Portugal? I'm assuming it's a place, but it might be a person, mightn't it? Some man named Carlos Manila who invented brown envelopes?

Oh God, it's like my head is getting sucked into a spin cycle . . . I can't write anymore, my hand is shaking . . .

. . .

Okay, I'm back. I did that meditation exercise my therapist taught me. I visualized a washing machine slowing down. I completely focus on watching it through the little glass window. I see the drum. It's making that clanking noise as it turns slower and slower. The spin cycle's ending. The drum comes to a complete halt. I watch it for a minute to make sure it doesn't move again.

Phew.

It's not exactly hard to see how nervous this is making me. Is it a bad idea? Should I just undo the manila envelope, rip open the one with the cash, and put it back in my wallet? And shred the other envelope?

I think about that, but the trouble is, when I imagine that picture it makes me feel even worse. Even more panicky and spin-cycley. And guilty. Much, much more guilty.

And as my therapist says, if there's one emotion that's really toxic for me, it's guilt.

Thirteen

"IT WASN'T YOUR FAULT"

God, I'm cross.

I've climbed back over the wall, which I didn't want to do: I wanted to ramble round the woods some more. Maybe take a leaf out of Taylor's book and climb a tree or two. But then if she caught a glimpse of me through the trees (she's right, this red T-shirt isn't exactly inconspicuous) and accused me of copying her, that would do my head in. It was bad enough being called a sneak without her adding "copycat" to the list of insults to throw at me.

I'm furious with Taylor. And I'm jealous of her drive and dedication. I don't have that iron discipline: if there's no one else there, I can't muster up the energy to make myself exercise. One of the reasons I depended on Ricky so much.

I'm more cross with myself than I am with Taylor, I realize. Because she's doing something she really enjoys, and I'm not. I go through the main school entrance and up to the Lower Sixth C classroom, thinking that, if I can't climb a rope, I can at least get my Latin grammar book and spend an hour learning some irregular verbs. I really need to make a huge effort in Latin, or I'll get chucked out of the class.

The classroom is completely empty. Outside I can hear the shrill cries of the third-formers at their skipping games. The first-formers are squeaking excitedly as they play French Elastic, in which two girls stand facing each other with a long loop of elastic round their ankles as a third jumps onto it and pulls it into increasingly complicated patterns. And, drumming along below the high-pitched screaming, there's the endless repetitive bounce of tennis balls thudding against the high stone terrace wall, punctuated by quick-fire rounds of what sounds like applause, as girls take turns to see how many times they can clap before catching the ball again. I *know*. Look, I never claimed Wakefield Hall was the height of metropolitan sophistication, did I?

The reason these incredibly old-fashioned schoolgirl games have survived here, as if Wakefield Hall were a living museum dedicated to the 1950s, is because there is *nothing to do* in the outside world between four p.m. when school gets out, and curfew time. Wakefield, the nearest suburb, is half an hour's walk down the main drive, and frankly, being a suburb, it lacks decent shops, cinemas, or anything that would really tempt a teenage girl. You have to get a tube for that, and by the time you've got to somewhere more interesting, it's five o'clock, say, and you have to leave by six on the dot to be sure of being back at seven for dinner. You really, really don't want to miss curfew. Grandmother—*Lady Wakefield*—throws you straight into solitary and makes you live on bread and water for a month. (I'm only slightly exaggerating.)

So a lot of girls just walk down the drive and have low-fat skim-milk cappuccinos in one of the Wakefield coffee shops. And those are the daring ones. Mostly girls just stock up on sweets and chocolate bars (and illicit drink, I'm sure) to vary the dull monotony of school food, and head right back up the drive again.

We do exchanges with the local boys' private school, for plays, sport, stuff like that, and the boarders can get weekend passes to stay with friends or family, but the bottom line is that at seven p.m., it's lockdown in Wakefield Hall Maximum Security Prison. All the day girls shoot out as soon as they can, unless they have orchestra or sports practice or something. Leaving the hapless boarders to entertain themselves as best they can with rousing rounds of French Elastic and Wall Ball.

Believe me, no one can pity us anymore than we pity ourselves.

I know the boarders have parties in their dormitories. I've heard the rumors. But it's not like anyone's going to invite me, is it? Having the headmistress's granddaughter over while you swill down cheap cider and watch naughty videos after lights-out isn't exactly a good security idea. So I sit alone in my room at Aunt Gwen's every night, staring at my computer screen, ignoring all the hate e-mails as best I can and downloading videos off YouTube. My Latin may be crap, but I'm still studying more than I ever did in my life, out of sheer tedium.

I wander over to the window and put my face to the glass. Some girls from the Lower Sixth—Meena, Jessica, and Susan, the class intellectuals—are clustered under the weeping willow tree on a slight hilly rise. They're studying together. Bloody swots. Don't they ever do anything fun? I think of the shiny, glossy St. Tabby's girls by the fountain, studying Advanced Grooming and Flirtation Skills, and I almost get a wave of nostalgia for how smooth and gorgeous they looked. At least at St. Tabby's there was something to aspire to. Here, the cleverer you are, the more you seem to feel the need to cultivate the grease in your hair and consider your blackheads a sign of extreme intellect, rather than God's way of telling you that you should get a better face wash.

Behind the three brainiacs, the trees gather densely, completely concealing the hedge maze so beloved by the younger girls, who spend hours chasing each other through it. I used to do that, too, in the summers we spent here visiting my grandmother, when school was out. I'd have friends round and we'd explore the grounds all day, taking sandwiches for lunch and coming back at sunset grass-stained, exhausted, and blissfully happy. That was when my parents were alive, of course. I haven't used the word *happy* to describe my emotional state much since the accident.

God, I'm being maudlin now. Things are bad enough

without me "dwelling," as my grandmother would say, and making them even worse. She does know what she's talking about every so often.

I turn away from the windows, walk over to my desk, and flick open the hinged top, which is pitted and scarred inside by generations of girls who've scratched and inked things onto the wood. But instead of fishing out my Latin books, I stand there, staring at the envelope lying on top of the pile.

Quite apart from the fact that it wasn't there the last time I opened my desk—putting books away at the end of my last class—there's something about it that's immediately perplexing. The writing on the front says `Scarlett Wakefield` in the oddest printing I've ever seen outside of a book. It looks like a robot wrote it. Or an android.

I may have been watching too many American sci-fi TV programs on my computer.

I hesitate for a moment, though I don't know why. Then I pick it up. It's sealed, and I need to rip it open. My heart is pounding for some reason. Inside is a single sheet of paper, with four words printed on it in the same weird typeface. Just four words. But they are the four words I have most longed to hear, the words no one ever said to me, and just seeing them printed on the white sheet of paper actually, I'm almost embarrassed to admit it, brings tears to my eyes.

`It wasn't your fault`

I sniff and look out the window and then back at the paper again, just to make sure I'm not hallucinating its message.

151

`It wasn't your fault`

I sniff again, and take a deep breath. Outside the screams and giggles and tennis-ball-bounce-and-clap are continuing, just as before, as if the world hadn't changed for me in the space of a moment.

I fold the paper up the way it was before and slide it back into the now jagged-edged envelope. My head is spinning.

In this split-second moment, everything has changed. I have a sense of purpose now.

I'll find out who left this for me if I die trying.

INCREDIBLY HOT GUY

I tear out of the classroom and actually burn rubber on the soles of my trainers as I do a scorching ninety-degree turn on the wooden floor of the corridor. I take the stairs not two, but three at a time, and when a gaggle of twelve-year-olds on the last flight are coming up as I'm flying down, I actually do that thing you see in films: I jump onto the banister and let my jeans-clad bum be pulled down it by gravity and the cunning sideways tilt of my buttocks, which gives me extra speed. Thank God the banister is old and highly polished. I'm going so fast I'd be worried about splinters otherwise.

The twelve-year-olds gasp in shock and awe as I whiz past them. I'm high. I'm flying. I'm Scarlett Wakefield and someone else besides me thinks that it *wasn't my fault*! I grab the newel post with my left hand, just as I'm about to hit it, and vault off the banister, hitting the ground running.

"*Scarlett Wakefield!*" calls a teacher from behind me.

"That's my name!" I sing. "Thank you for caring!"

I don't think she hears me, because I'm long gone by

then, out the door and zooming around the side of the school, through the courtyard, scattering rope-skippers, sending the two French Elastic players with the elastic round their ankles tripping as they swivel round to see who's sprinting as if she has the devil on her heels. Past the weeping willow, where the swots turn to stare at me— they've probably never had a good run in their lives. Round the outside of the maze, skirting Lime Walk, and onto the Great Lawn, aka the hockey pitches, which are still green and grassy, not the slicks of mud they'll be after Sharon Persaud and her psycho friends have had a go at it with it with their cleats and killer sticks. I tumble down the steep slope from Lime Walk and as I hit the lawn I use the momentum I've built up and run hard, one two three lunge and push into a handspring, which has such a good landing that I go mad and throw in a bounder straight afterward, which, to be honest, I barely land without doing myself a serious injury.

Three months off gymnastics, and I'm tumbling on grass in trainers. I must be insane. Especially doing a bounder. It's like a handspring, only you jump into it with both feet together, which is much harder than lunging and kicking into it. People who have freakishly strong legs don't have any problems with bounders. But if you don't, you have to work really hard to make it over without landing ignominiously on your bum. When my hands hit the grass, I shove the ground away with everything I've got, popping my shoulders as much as I can, and it's just enough to get me over and back to my feet again.

My head is spinning, and it's not the tumbling that's done it. I am high on pure joy. There isn't a drug in the world that's worth one gram of my own adrenaline (I didn't make that up; it's a Ricky-ism).

Also, I'm very relieved that I didn't just break an ankle. I stand there, panting, when I hear clapping. I turn round, and a rook flies out of one of the linden trees, cawing loudly. Oh. No applause. Just a bird beating its wings. My shoulders sag. I was actually hoping, pathetically, that someone had seen me and spontaneously burst into—

I look further down the avenue of trees, and see him. That gardener boy again, piling leaves into a wheelbarrow. Only he's put down his rake, and he's walking toward me, down the slope. Clapping.

"Hey," I say, still catching my breath.

He's beaming at me. He has a lovely smile. And I know this is going to sound crazy, but, as he gets closer, I suddenly realize that he's drop-dead gorgeous. He has butterscotch skin, a head of short black curls so tight they look as if they were each made by winding them round a knitting needle, and eyes of such a light, bright hazel that they seem almost gold. I remember when I met him before I thought that eye color was a trick of the light. Well, it isn't. His eyes really are that golden. He must be biracial, with hair like that and skin that toffee color.

Wow. I stand there and goggle at him. I can't believe I didn't notice before how handsome he was. His teeth are incredibly white against his caramel skin. I feel very self-conscious about mine by comparison. And suddenly I'm aware of how old and faded my red T-shirt is, how unfashionable my jeans and trainers are, and that when I was upside down he must have seen a bit of my tummy, which isn't half as flat and toned as Taylor's is. It's genetics, I know, but I'd still kill to have a flatter tummy.

"I didn't know you did gymnastics," he says, and then looks a bit embarrassed himself. "Well, why would I. That's a stupid thing to say . . . "

He tails off, and I find myself jumping in to keep the conversation going. "Ever since I was small."

"You must have won a lot of prizes."

I laugh. "Oh, I'm not that good. Anyway, that was nothing. You should see me when I've got a proper spring floor to bounce off."

And then I catch myself, realizing that I sound like I'm boasting. I *am* boasting. What's he supposed to say to that?

"Well, I thought it looked really cool," he says.

It's a warm day, and he's wearing loose jeans and a bright green T-shirt that's pretty much plastered to him. He's worked up a sweat, raking leaves and pushing the wheelbarrow, and I can see that though he's pretty lean, he's not skinny. I remember noticing his forearms before, which are bulging and corded from hard physical labor. But now I look up and see how wide his shoulders are, how capped they are with muscle.

I realize I'm staring, and I feel a blush flooding my cheeks.

"You're all pink," he comments, smiling again. "You were really racing along there."

"I didn't see you," I say, very glad that he's misinterpreted my blush.

"I'm just the invisible man where you're concerned, aren't I?" he says, looking me straight in the eye. "I waved to you earlier, when I was pruning the hedge over by the rose garden, but I don't think you saw me."

I stare back into his eyes, golden and glowing in the afternoon sunlight. I've never seen a color like that before. It's mesmerising. *He's* mesmerising.

"My name's Jase, by the way," he adds, rubbing his hand on his jeans and reaching it out to me. "Short for Jason. My granddad's the head gardener here. Old Ted."

"You're *Ted Barnes's* grandson?"

My eyes widen. Ted Barnes is wizened, ancient, and definitely one hundred percent white, with a face covered in broken veins from gardening in all sorts of weather, and, my aunt Gwen says darkly, a drinking habit to boot. His grandson couldn't look less like him if he were actively trying.

Completely unoffended, Jason Barnes grins.

"Not that much alike, are we? Lucky for me. Grandad's no oil painting."

He's still holding out his hand. I grab at it, feeling I've

made him wait too long, and as I touch it, I don't understand why he even needed to wipe it. He's dry as a bone, his palm rough from the work of gardening, and I can feel calluses studding the base of his fingers. Without thinking, I touch them with the pad of my index finger.

He jerks his hand away. It's the first awkward gesture or movement I've seen from him.

"I shouldn't have shaken hands," he blurts, shoving his into his pockets. "Mine are all cracked. Sorry, it's all the digging."

I think he's blushing, though it's harder to tell on him than on me.

"I've got those, too," I jump in quickly. "Look."

Three months have diminished my calluses a bit, but they've been built up by years of training, and you don't lose that kind of thing overnight. I turn my hands over to show him my palms.

"God, you do as well," he says in surprise.

"Asymmetric bars and rope climbing," I explain. "If the calluses get big you have to pumice them down, or they really hurt when you're holding on to something. They dig into you."

"I pick mine off," Jase admits, grinning.

I can't believe we're bonding over calluses. How weird is that?

Jase takes my hands in his. My whole body fizzes at the contact as if I'm radioactive. My hands rest in his larger ones, on his palms, which are a pale pink gray edged by caramel, and are much, much bigger than mine.

"You've got tiny hands," he says. "I'm amazed they can hold you up when you're upside down like that."

I laugh, and then I hear the sound I'm making. It's not a laugh. It's a full-on girly giggle.

I am giggling with a boy.

Now it's my turn to pull my hands away, though not as fast as he did. I stand there and look at Jase, at his wide shoulders and his bright golden eyes, and I feel a rush of excitement flood through me.

"Are you okay?" he asks curiously.

I swallow hard. "Yeah, I just need to get back. I've got to do some revision, there's this test tomorrow . . ."

"Oh, okay then." Jase looks a bit disappointed and it makes me grin a little. "See you round?"

"Definitely."

"At least you know my name now, eh?"

"Jase," I say, and my voice comes out wobbly, to my great embarrassment.

"That's right," he says, quite seriously. "Don't you go forgetting it, now."

"I won't."

I turn away and start walking across the Great Lawn, taking a shortcut through the grounds to the gatekeeper's cottage.

"Scarlett?" Jase calls after me.

I turn round and look at him.

"Good luck with the test!" he yells.

I can only manage a wave and then I break into another run, not because I'm in any hurry to get back to Aunt Gwen's, but because there are so many feelings inside of me that I'm scared I'll explode all over the Great Lawn.

After a few minutes, I stop for a minute at a bench and take a deep breath. What I need right now is some time by myself, alone in my room. At the end there, talking to Jase, I got sort of overloaded, like a computer just before it crashes, because I suddenly found myself being reminded of Dan. Dan was really impressed when he saw me do gymnastics. Just like Jase. And while the circumstances were different—I was deliberately showing off for Dan, and I didn't know Jase was there when I threw myself into that handspring bounder—it still felt weird, like déjà vu.

My brain flashed to that night outside on Nadia's terrace, and I couldn't quite deal with it. I had to run away and get some space, find somewhere to be alone so I could sort through all of my emotions, which are completely at war with one another—happy shock over the note, excitement from talking with Jase, sadness at the thought of Dan. It's all a blur.

I begin running toward home again. I weave through the ornamental garden, round the hedge (which is looking nicely trimmed, I notice: good work, Jase), and arrive at our front door. It's unlocked. Aunt Gwen is in. But there's one very positive side to living with Aunt Gwen: like Lady

Severs, she wants to see as little of me as possible. She may be large and pale and have big buggy eyes like a frog's, but she never comes near me unless it's absolutely necessary. I can just about see her shoulder—she's in her study, as she pretty much always is, sitting at her desk—but she doesn't turn round as I come in, let alone say a "Hi" or acknowledge me in any way.

That's fine. It's just the way I like it. For years, Aunt Gwen and I have basically pretended that the other one doesn't exist. It's a system that has worked very well for both of us and neither of us sees any reason to mess with it now. I run upstairs and into my room, closing the door behind me. For an instant, I shut my eyes. Peace and quiet, I think.

A chance to look again at that note (which is shoved deep into my jeans pocket) and see what deductions I can draw from it. A chance to absorb the impact of meeting Jase Barnes again and properly *seeing* him. A chance to feel again the incredible sensation of him taking my hands in his and saying how small they were.

Heat rushes over me as I remember Dan kissing me on Nadia's terrace, and my heart is beating so loudly, I think I can actually hear it.

But suddenly I hear a crashing noise, which is certainly not my heart beating.

My eyes snap open. I sweep a quick look round the room and realize that it's not as I left it. My folder with all the articles about Dan and me is lying on my bed, open. The articles are scattered all over the bed. Some have blown to the floor because there's a breeze coming in from the window, which I'm sure I didn't leave wide open this morning . . .

I run to the window and look out.

That's where the noise was coming from. Someone was in my room. And now they're—I lean further out and look down—*climbing down the drainpipe*, which is rattling as it's knocked against the wall by her weight.

I don't need to identify the shock of shaggy hair directly below me.

It's Taylor. Taylor was in my room, spying on me.

Any wish for a moment of peace and quiet has gone in a flash. I vault up onto the windowsill, look for my mark, take a deep breath, and jump out of the window.

fifteen

BEING TARZAN

I know I'm going to catch the branch. When you've spent as much time as I have swinging from one asymmetric bar to the other, you're not worried about your aim. What I don't know—and this is the big question—is whether the branch will bear my weight.

I always used to climb out of this window when I was smaller, and under curfew, by crawling along the big branch of the oak tree just behind Aunt Gwen's house. I could still do that, but by the time I'd crawled along it and climbed from one branch to another, down the trunk of the tree, Taylor would be long gone.

So I have to improvise. There's a smaller, whippier branch a foot below the big one, narrow enough for me to get a grip on it. I launch myself toward it, aiming as close to the trunk as I can, because it'll be stronger there, and as soon as my fingers clasp round the branch, I let it take all my weight for one split second, and then I kick forward, swing back good and high, and launch myself yet again in a long powerful swing that sends me flying through the air, feet reaching out, arms stretching back, making myself as long and as aerodynamic as possible, so that I land on the thick lush grass yards and yards beyond the tree.

It's as soft a landing as I could have hoped for. I don't even stumble: I hit the ground running. Taylor's only a few feet in front of me and as she looks back, gobsmacked to see me so close to her, she loses a precious second or two gaping at me in amazement.

I've got to give it to her: she recovers quickly and snaps her head round again, pumping those super-strong legs, sprinting away from my pursuit. But I have the wind in my sails, and, just as important, I know these grounds so well I could run through them blindfolded. Taylor has barely been at school for a couple of weeks. And it swiftly becomes apparent that she has no idea where she's going, apart from Away From Me.

I bide my time, keeping pace with Taylor, and the moment I see her hesitate, I pounce. She's just rounded the corner of a hedge, and there's the ornamental garden to her left, another hedge stretching away on her right. Taylor doesn't know which way will be faster. In the moment that she wavers, I speed up, zooming toward her, and as she realizes what's happening I spring at her, grabbing the back of her T-shirt, crashing into her and forcing her to fall to the ground under me.

Taylor lands really well. She rolls, tucking her head in, and if it weren't for having me on her back, she'd have been able to roll right over and come to her feet easily enough. But I've thought this through—I've sent her crashing into the hedge, and I have her trapped between me and a face full of nasty spiky branches. If she doesn't want her face torn off, she won't struggle. And her arms, in that tank top, are bare: she won't want to get them cut up. I keep her wedged in there, half-sitting on her. We're both sweaty, but I'm used to spotting other girls in gymnastics, and being this close to someone else's sweaty body doesn't freak me out. I put my weight on her to stop her escaping.

"What the hell were you doing in my room?" I ask, my breath coming in big gasps.

Taylor is not as breathless as I am, which I find deeply annoying.

"How did you get out of there so fast?" she asks, her chest heaving but her voice sounding only curious. "Did you just jump out the window?"

"Of course not! I'd have broken both my ankles!"

"Then how did you *do* that? You couldn't have climbed down the drainpipe, you would have been miles behind me!"

"I swung off a branch." God, I make it sound like I'm Tarzan.

Taylor's green eyes widen. "Jeez!" she exclaims. "Have you done that before?"

"No."

"Then how did you know it'd hold your weight?"

"I didn't."

"Wow," she says, her eyes widening further.

This is ridiculous. I just caught this girl going through my most private stuff, chased her out of my window, and rugby-tackled her to the ground, and now I'm actually *flattered* that she thinks I'm some kind of minor super-heroine.

"You can let me out from under this bush." Taylor tries to turn her head away from the branches in her face. "I won't run away."

"How do I know you won't?" I ask.

I couldn't beat her in a fight. No way. Look at those rope-climbing muscles. Taylor is probably twice as strong as I am. My only advantage now is that she's trapped under the hedge.

"Where would I go?" Taylor points out. "You'd only catch me again if I ran. You know this place way better than I do. Besides, you could turn me in to your grandma."

I stare at her, thinking this over. I can see that Taylor's right. Eventually—I don't want to give in too easily and make her think I'm a pushover—I nod begrudgingly and release my grip on her. She wiggles out from under the hedge and sits up cross-legged, wiping leaves and her messy fringe off her face. I realize that I have become distracted from the main issue here, which of course is Taylor's breaking and entering.

"How dare you break into my room!" I shout.

"I'm sorry," she says simply.

"You don't look sorry."

"Well, it was sort of fun climbing up the drainpipe and getting in," Taylor admits.

I can completely see that it would be a lot of fun, but that is Not The Point.

"You looked through my private stuff! That is so . . . wrong!" I'm practically seething with anger now.

"Yeah, that was bad," she says. She looks straight at me. "You gonna tell anyone?"

Oh, I hate her. Hate her. Because she already knows the answer somehow, I can see it in her face. And she's cut right to it—she hasn't gone through the ritual of apologizing, explaining, asking me for forgiveness, pleading with me not to tell, all the polite back-and-forth that would make me feel that she'd done some penance for invading my privacy.

"I ought to tell my grandmother right away." The tone of my voice is sharp and curt, just like Lady Wakefield's.

"But you won't," Taylor says slowly, as if she's confirming something to herself.

I narrow my eyes at her.

"You're really pushing your luck," I snap.

"Yeah, whatever," Taylor says with a sarcastic roll of the eyes. "I suppose you want to hear me say I'm sorry or something."

I can't believe how bitchy she's being, and how smart. I didn't tell on her just now, and she's calculating that I won't do it this time either. But she's brave enough to take the risk that I *will* tell, so she's apparently not even afraid of expulsion. I'd admire that quality in her if she hadn't just snooped through my things. "No, I want to know why you were in my room."

"I don't know, okay?" Taylor snaps. "Look, I shouldn't have done it. Anyway, I didn't see anything important."

Instinctively, I know she's lying. But for some reason I also know that she won't tell anyone what she found. Because if Taylor can recognize that I'm not a sneak. I can see the same quality in her. Both of us fight our own battles:

167

we don't go running to teachers or anyone else to sort things out for us. We're both lone warriors. Takes one to know one.

I lever myself up off the grass and wipe off the seat of my jeans. Taylor, sensibly, doesn't follow suit; she stays sitting there, looking up at me, waiting for my next move.

"Stay away from me from now on." I point a finger at her and fix her with my best scary stare. "If I ever catch you near my stuff again, you will regret it. That's a promise."

I don't wait for her to say anything. I just turn on my heel and walk away across the grass. I'm still pissed off, but it's good to have had the last word. Refocusing my attention on the note, I come to the conclusion that although Taylor is a nasty cow who broke into my room, she wasn't the one who left that envelope in my desk. Taylor only just this minute searched my room, and the note was left for me at least an hour or so ago—probably when Taylor was busy climbing trees. From her sweaty state, she looked as if she'd been in that forest for a good long time. She didn't have either the knowledge about me—or, from her hostile attitude just now, the empathy—to write a sentence like "It wasn't your fault." And most likely, she didn't have the opportunity to leave the note.

So I can definitely rule her out. Not that that helps much. One girl down, a couple of hundred to go. I need to think very carefully indeed about how to find out who left that note.

I need to set a trap.

sixteen

COMPLETELY COVERED IN INK

"Oh my God!" I stare down into my open desk. It's the day after I found the envelope, and I spent all yesterday evening thinking up a Cunning Plan. So here I am, executing it. "Bloody hell, I don't _believe_ it!"

Sharon Persaud (of the killer lavender hockey stick), who has the desk next to me, turns to look.

"What's wrong?" she asks.

"There's ink all over my books! I don't know how that happened!"

"Is everything okay?"

"No! God, look at this!" I pick up an ink-sodden enve-lope and the notebook below it, and wave them both around. "They're completely soaked!"

Meena, who sits behind me, leans forward.

"How did that happen?" she asks.

"I dunno . . ." I rifle through the contents of the desk with my other hand. "There was this pen on top, it must have leaked all over my Latin notes, and this other stuff. God, it's all *ruined*. I'm going to have to chuck it all out."

Meena is fishing in her own desk.

"Here," she says, handing me a pack of Kleenex. "And you can borrow my Latin notes, Scarlett."

"Wow, really?"

I turn to look fully at her. Her expression is very sympathetic. Meena's not very attractive. She's unhealthy-looking, skinny, and pale-skinned for a girl of Indian descent, which makes the dark circles under her eyes even more evident, giving her a slightly raccoonlike appearance. But her smile now is very friendly.

"Thanks so much," I say. The notebook doesn't contain my Latin notes, of course: it's blank. But I wouldn't at all mind borrowing Meena's Latin notes. They're bound to be better than mine.

"Can you read *anything*, Scarlett?" asks Susan, another girl from my Latin class.

"No," I say hopelessly. "It's completely covered in ink. And it's gone right through to whatever's inside. Bloody pen, I don't believe this happened!"

"Yeah, that's really unlucky," chimes in Lizzie, the scared girl from gymnastics with the un–Wakefield Hall–like highlights in her hair. "I had that happen to me once in my rucksack. My iPod cover got completely messed up. I had to throw it away. And it was a really nice one, too."

There's a chorus of sympathy. I must say, girls at Wakefield Hall are a lot nicer than the ones at St. Tabby's.

They may be wary of me because my grandmother's the headmistress, but in a genuine crisis, they all demonstrate that they're fully-paid-up members of the human race. If this had happened at St. Tabby's, only my immediate friends would have gathered round to coo and empathize. No one else would have cared. Unless it had happened to Plum, or one of her inner circle. In that case, it would have been played for as much drama as possible, and tons of sycophants would have crowded around Plum all day long, as she threw her hair around and pouted and played the situation for the maximum amount of attention.

"What's all this noise about?" Miss Newman booms from the doorway.

We all jump. Miss Newman's voice is like a bass drum, cutting through all the chatter with deep, terrifying authority.

I open my mouth to explain, but to my surprise, Meena cuts in first.

"Please, Miss Newman, Scarlett's had a pen leak in her desk," she says.

Miss Newman's phenomenally hairy eyebrows draw together so tightly they actually meet in a monobrow that wouldn't look out of place on a Greek wrestler.

"Very careless to leave your pens lying loose, Scarlett," she says. "If they'd been in a pencil case, this wouldn't have happened, would it?"

My eyes roll despite myself. What *decade* does she think we're living in? Who has *pencil cases* anymore?

"Don't pull faces at me, young lady!" Miss Newman shouts. "Now go and wash your hands! You've barely got five minutes before morning assembly!"

"Here," offers Susan. She pulls a plastic bag out of her desk, takes some stuff out of it and hands it along the row. "You can put the inky stuff in there, Scarlett," she suggests. "That way it won't go all over everything else."

"Thanks, Susan," I say gratefully, taking the bag.

Susan blushes and ducks her head. She's extraordinarily pretty, but I don't think she knows it. She never wears any makeup, nor does anything with her pale blond hair other than scrape it back into a tight ponytail. She actually reminds me a little bit of Luce, now I look at her more closely. Susan, like Luce, has a little-girl quality to her that conceals a very sharp mind. They both have a fragility that tends to make people—even teachers who ought to know better—underestimate how clever they are.

God, I miss Luce and Alison, so much that it's like a physical pain. It's these flashes of memory that hurt the most, the reminders of friends I've lost through my own bad behavior.

But I can't think about anything now but the job at hand. I chuck the bag with the inky things into the dustbin, and nip out of the room and down the corridor to the big tiled loo to wash my hands. I don't get them completely clean, though. I leave a good amount of ink still staining my fingers, enough so I can flash them around and complain, at every possible opportunity, about the leaky pen that ruined tons of stuff in my desk. Which will be Part A of Operation Inky Envelope successfully concluded. I check myself in the mirror. I've managed to get a small ink stain on my nose, which is perfect. Everyone will ask me about it.

I know it sounds tragic. But believe me, if I spend the next few hours showing everyone the ink stains on my hands and whingeing about them, everyone will be discussing Scarlett's Ink-Stain Misery. Not because it's interesting in any way, shape, or form, but because there's nothing else to talk about in this underage girls' prison.

Okay, that's not quite true. There's definitely something hot to talk about here, and his name is Jase Barnes. Mmm. I find myself picturing his wide shoulders, remembering the way he took my hands, and a rush of heat rises up through me and settles in my lower stomach and I start grinning like a lunatic. Before I know it something hard and cold bumps into my forehead. And I realize that I just went so moony over Jase Barnes that I must have leant forward in a daze, over the sink, until my forehead hit the mirror.

I pull back, giggling a bit. Wow, I'm being such an idiot: just picturing Jase turns me to complete and utter mush. I have to pull myself together. I have to find out who left me that note, and what's behind it, and how Dan died, before I can even *think* about Jase in any leaning-forward-toward-him-to-be-kissed kind of way . . .

Oh God, Dan. The giggles dissolve immediately. I look at myself in the mirror and see a guilty face staring back at me. Am I obsessed with solving the mystery of how Dan died just so I can go right out and kiss another boy without worrying that he'll drop down dead at my feet? Am I making it all about me?

But it isn't, or it shouldn't be. It's about Dan. How he died. And who was responsible. Because if someone left me that note, it means that there's more to this than came out at the inquest. At least one person knows more than they're telling. And I'm not going to let things rest till I find out who they are and what really happened that night on Nadia's terrace. I think about his family, and how upset they must be. I remember his parents being at the inquest, but I was so out of it with my own misery and confusion that I don't remember them; I can't picture them; I have no image of what they look like. But it must be the worst thing in the world to have your son dead and not even know how it happened.

And right now, it looks as if I'm the only person with any chance of finding the answer to that mystery.

Because whoever was responsible certainly isn't telling.

seventeen

"EVERYTHING HAPPENS FOR A REASON"

The double bell, signifying classes are over for the day, rings at four. After that, the classroom wing stays open till six-thirty, for people doing extra classes or needing to get things from their desks. Then it's locked up till eight-fifteen the next morning.

So Part B of Operation Inky Envelope is tightly structured. I'm going to surveil (if that's a word) my desk during lunch break and from four to six-thirty every evening. The rest of the time—before school starts, during class changeovers—I'll be in the classroom, lurking close to my desk at all times, making sure no one slips something into it. Wakefield Hall is so old-fashioned that we still have the ancient wooden desks with lift-up tops and deep inside wells in which we store most of our books and notes. The students don't move from classroom to classroom, unless we're doing science and need to go to the lab; the teachers come to us, which means that we're always sitting at the same desk, with all the stuff we need directly available. It's not a terrible system. There are lockers downstairs for valuables, in the changing rooms where we hang our coats and gym stuff, but I don't have a locker. I don't need one, living so tragically close to school as I do.

So that makes things very simple. If whoever left the envelope wants to leave me a second one, to make sure I got their message, they'll have to leave it in my desk, like they did before. Aunt Gwen's house is far enough away from the parts of the grounds where the girls are allowed to go to make it too risky for someone to put a note through the front door. And clearly the note-leaver doesn't want to trust the post—they want to make absolutely sure that I get the envelope. So, my desk it is—during lunch break or after school, because those are the only opportunities they'll have.

Sending them straight into my cunning trap.

The only trouble is, I have to get into it, too.

I put my books into my desk, taking my time doing it. When I've finished, the classroom has practically cleared out. One of the good things about my desk being against the far wall is that I can linger at it until everyone else has left the room, making sure that no one can slip anything into it when my back's turned. I wait till everyone else has long gone, and only then do I leave the classroom.

Unlike everyone else, I don't go toward the main stairs. Instead, I turn away and walk down the corridor in the direction no one wants to take this time of day unless they have to—the teachers' block. It's strictly out of bounds, unless you're being called in there to be hauled over the carpet by some teacher—or, worst of all, by my grandmother, whose palatial rooms stretch over the first floor of the building.

To picture Wakefield Hall's layout, imagine a capital *E*. Then take out the middle stroke of the *E*. What's left is the shape of the main building, the ancient, historical, dating-back-to-the-sixteenth-century one. The schoolrooms are in the left-hand wing; the assembly hall-slash-theater, plus the teachers' flats and my grandmother's grand suite of rooms, are in the long main part, and the other wing, well, that's where I'm going. Because the top two floors of the other wing are abandoned. My grandmother would call them "unoccupied," but "abandoned" is what they are.

She wanted to make them into a big flat for my parents and me, when my dad eventually decided to move back here from London. And then my parents died, and that was the end of that plan. I don't like to think about that—what my life would have been like if my parents hadn't died in that accident. What can't be cured must be endured, as my grandmother would say.

Still, she hasn't exactly recovered from it either. Because she hasn't touched that part of the building since then. It's completely closed off.

I doubt she's even been in it.

I run up the stairs that lead to the top floor of the teachers' wing. I know it's pretty unlikely I'll bump into a teacher here this time of day—they're all supervising play time, or teaching after-school special classes. Sure enough, there's nobody around. I nip along the corridor until I reach the parallel staircase on the other side of the building, and the door that leads to the far wing. It's padlocked shut. No going through there. So I have to use the window at the top of the staircase, which overlooks the fire escape.

When I was checking this out yesterday, I didn't want to open the door to the fire escape. It has a big ALARMED sign on it in red. So I boost myself up onto the window ledge, swing open the window—one of those old-fashioned ones that hinges open like a door—and climb through, onto the fire escape. I push the window nearly shut behind me, enough to look like it's completely closed, but open just a crack, so that when I come back I can slip a finger between the window and the frame and ease it open for me to get back inside.

And then I'm on the fire escape stairs, scampering up them to the roof, climbing over and dropping down behind the big stone castellations (Wakefield Hall, despite its name, has some very castlelike features). Phew. I breathe an enormous sigh of relief. Climbing out the window, being in open sight on the fire escape, a place that's completely and utterly out of bounds to any student, even if she's the headmistress's granddaughter, is the most dangerous part of this entire escapade. Now I'm on the roof, hidden behind the battlements, no one can see me.

Still, I don't have time to congratulate myself. I need to get into place as quickly as possible, in case envelope-delivery is already taking place in Lower Sixth C. If I only had an accomplice, this would be so much easier. I could have her hang around the classroom, making sure anyone who wanted to slip an envelope into my desk would have to wait till she was gone, to give me enough time to get to my observation point. It's so much harder planning and carrying this all out on my own. I dash across the roof to the skylight, which I levered open yesterday, and is cracked ajar a bit by the rope that's tied to its hinge. I lift it up, grunting with the effort—it's leaded glass and it weighs a *ton*—and lower it down to lie on the roof. Then I uncoil the rope and drop it down into the room below. And then I sit down on the edge, my feet dangling into the room, take a good grip on the rope, and swing myself off into empty space.

Every time I do this, I think I'm going to fall, that my arms won't hold me. Every time. I hang there for a long, scary moment, my feet scrabbling to find the rope, my right leg trying to hook around it to bring my right foot into position underneath it so my left foot can grab onto the rope and sandwich it between my feet to take some of my body weight . . . Ow, my hands hurt . . . my arms are aching with the drop and the strain of holding me up . . . my feet feel completely uncoordinated . . . the rope keeps slipping out of the hook of my right knee . . .

And then I've got it. Phew. Now my feet are in place, it's infinitely easier. I lower myself down, hand over hand, feet taking enough weight so I don't get rope burn, and drop lightly to the floor. I cross the huge, empty room to the window that looks onto the classroom wing. And there it is, across from me: the window of Lower Sixth C, with my desk right next to it.

Aunt Gwen used to drive me mad by saying "Everything happens for a reason." God, how I hate that expression. People only use it when something bad has happened to you, and it never makes you feel any better. I did notice that the one thing that Aunt Gwen did *not* say "Everything happens for a reason" about was Dan's death. Even she didn't manage to put a pious spin on that.

But now, reluctantly, those very words are ringing in my head. As I pick up Aunt Gwen's bird-watching binoculars, which I brought in yesterday, and hold them in front of my eyes, focusing on my desk by the window (one of the worst desks in the room, because its owner is trapped at the far end of a front row), I wonder if maybe everything *does* happen for a reason, as now I can focus perfectly on my desk, which is in full view—the *best* desk in the room for surveillance purposes . . .

There's always the chance that someone already nipped back into the classroom and sneaked a replacement envelope into my desk. But hopefully they haven't done that yet. Hopefully they'll be waiting till the floor empties out, and it's nice and quiet, with much less chance of anyone else entering the classroom just as they lift the lid of my desk and slide that envelope in . . .

So I curl up as best as I can on the windowsill, and keep watching.

My hands cramp on the binoculars. My feet go to sleep. My legs get pins and needles.

No matter how much I shift position, I can't get comfortable on this hard, cold stone windowsill.

Half an hour goes by. And still there's no one in the classroom. Bored, I start to train the binoculars on other windows, and then on the school grounds, checking back on the window next to my desk every minute or so just to make sure I don't miss anything. Oh wow . . . Jase Barnes! When I'm sitting at that desk, I spend so much time looking out the window, trying to spot him. And now I've got my wish: I'm looking at him, and he doesn't know. Spying on him feels weird, naughty, and wrong, but exciting at the same time. He's walking round the side of the new extension, the big ugly wing my grandmother added in the seventies. Ted Barnes's cottage is back there, off behind the new building, so maybe that's where he's coming from.

It's the first time I've seen Jase out of work clothes: he's in jeans and a bright blue shirt that fits him really nicely, and as he strides, his steps long and loose, across the drive and in through the side door of Wakefield Hall, he looks so gorgeous that I completely forget that I'm supposed to be watching my classroom. Only when he disappears from view do I realize what I'm actually here for and guiltily whip the binoculars back to the classroom window again. Also, I realize that my mouth is actually hanging open. I may even be drooling a bit.

Ooh, movement—someone in the classroom! I frantically focus on them, hoping to God that I haven't missed anything while I was ogling Jase. It's Lizzie. She's carrying the most awful handbag—it's gigantic and puke-green, glinting with gold studs and tassels and buckles and decorative padlocks. I'm sure it's the latest in designer clothes, but that doesn't make it any less ugly. Lizzie looks exactly like a low-grade pupil at St. Tabby's. She reminds me of the girls further down the social scale who slavishly copy everything that Plum and Nadia and Venetia wear, but who are just clones, without a personality or style of their own.

Lizzie dumps the horrible handbag down onto her desk, and stares at it for a moment. Oh my God, I think, is it Lizzie? Is she about to reach inside it and pull out a replacement note for me? Then she does something really unexpected. She sits down behind her desk, puts her arms on it, pushing the bag away, and drops her head between her arms. For a moment I can't work out what's happening. Then I focus in tighter on her body, and realize that her shoulders are bobbing up and down. She's crying. Maybe she's just realized how much money she threw away on that atrocity of a bag.

I'm joking to make light of the fact that, truthfully, there's something that creeps me out about silently watching someone else cry. I feel like a voyeur of someone else's pain, and I don't like it. I want to put down the binoculars, but I can't, because of the very slim chance that it might be Lizzie after all, having a sob before she pulls herself together and leaves me another note after all . . .

I sigh. My attention slips from crying Lizzie, to wonder instead what Jase is doing in the Wakefield Hall main building. Reporting to my grandmother on the grounds maintenance, I assume, or something equally dull. But my imagination runs away with me, and I picture Jase taking his time as he walks through the school, on the alert to see if he'll bump into me, and causing a raging hormonal stir in every girl he passes . . . God, I'm being an idiot to think that Jase might be on the lookout for me. He could have his pick of any girl here, and he probably flirts with anyone who crosses his path.

There's more movement in the classroom. I snap my attention back, and when I see who's just entered, I suck my breath in sharply.

It's Taylor.

She takes in the scene in front of her, and says something. I see her lips move. Lizzie raises her head and turns to look at Taylor. I can't see her face, but she must have said something, and something funny, to boot, because Taylor bursts out laughing. Weird. Why is Lizzie crying one minute and making jokes the next? Then Lizzie pushes her chair back and jumps up. She's gesturing, her head is jerking back and forth: it looks like she's shouting at Taylor.

Taylor is frowning now, snapping out some sort of response, which just seems to wind Lizzie up further. She's pointing at Taylor, her head's still wobbling . . . I guess that she's still yelling. I am so frustrated I can't read lips! But even if I could, I'd only get one side of the interchange, because all I can see is the back of Lizzie's head.

What are they arguing about? What could fashion-victim Lizzie and butch, tree-climbing Taylor possibly have to argue about?

My mind is racing with excitement and speculation, so

much that I actually jump when another shape walks into the twin circles of my binoculars. I pull back quickly, fiddling to get this new actor in the scene in focus. It's Meena. Yawn. Meena's the archetypal Wakefield Hall girl, a dowdy brainiac whose only aim seems to be to pass as many exams as possible. How my grandmother would love a school full of girls just like her, with her lank hair, baggy cords, oversize fluffy sweater and equally oversize brain. Meena's arms hang awkwardly by her sides and she stands there, looking confused at the fight going on in the classroom.

Still, Meena . . . could she be the one who left the note? I remember how nice she was to me when I pulled that ink-stained envelope out of my desk, how concerned she was, how she leaned forward. I thought she was being caring, but maybe she was trying to see how stained the envelope actually was, whether her message inside was still readable. And for Meena, who sits behind me, it would be pretty easy to leave a note in my desk.

But why on earth would Meena leave me a message like that? What could dowdy, un-chic Meena know about anything that happened at a super cool St. Tabby's party?

Meena's saying something, looking back and forth between Taylor and Lizzie. Lizzie waves her arms about again. Taylor shrugs, her expression bored. Lizzie flops back down into the chair again and sinks her head in her arms once more. I tilt the binoculars, fiddling again with the focus, trying to keep all three girls in view.

Just then, Taylor's head turns toward the windows and

for a second she's looking directly at me, those green eyes meeting mine. Even though I know she can't possibly see me—I'm too far away—it's a shock. I jump, and the binoculars slip momentarily in my suddenly sweaty hands. And then Taylor turns on her heel and walks quickly out of the classroom. Had she come in to leave the note? Was she so frustrated to find Lizzie there that she said something that made Lizzie angry? And why is she walking out without saying another word?

Meena pulls up a chair to sit next to Lizzie, puts her arm round Lizzie's shoulders, and hands her some tissues to dry her eyes. Lizzie raises her head, dabbing at her face with the tissues. They talk for a while, their heads close together. Then they stand up. Lizzie gathers up her nasty green bag, and they walk toward the door. Lizzie's ahead.

And then Meena stops by her desk. She opens the lid, and my heart slams. Is this it? Did she come in to leave that note; is it in her desk, is she about to fish it out and put it in mine? Lizzie's left the classroom by now. Meena is completely unobserved, as far as she knows.

But no such luck. The lid goes down again and all Meena has in her hands are a couple of books—probably what she came into the classroom to get. She's going out. That's it. All that drama for nothing. No note left. It's not Meena.

My shoulders sag in disappointment.

Then Lizzie darts back inside again. Her mouth is moving, her head's turned toward the door, she's saying something—to

185

Meena, I assume, who is still invisible. My heart is suddenly pounding: is this it? Is it Lizzie? She's moving fast across the room, going straight for my desk—no, no, she isn't, she's going toward Meena's, which is just behind mine. She's picking up the pack of tissues, which Meena left on her desk. She's taking the tissues and slipping them into her bag.

It's not Lizzie.

And then I gasp. Because Lizzie, passing my desk on her way out, the tissues tucked away, is pulling out something else from her bag. A white envelope. In one smooth movement, she cracks open my desk lid with one hand and slides in the envelope with the other, never slowing her stride.

It's Lizzie.

She's gone. Oh my God. I can't believe I actually saw it happen! My plan worked! I'm fizzing with excitement. I stay watching the room for another ten minutes or so. It's an effort even to hold the binoculars straight, I'm so excited now. But I wait and watch for a while, because that's the good super-spy thing to do.

Also, I'm sure that if I tried to climb the rope back up to the roof in my advanced state of excitement, fizzing with ideas about how to confront Lizzie and get the truth from her, I would be so buzzy that I would slip, fall off, break my ankle, and lie here in a deserted room padlocked from the outside till I starved to death.

I really ought to start carrying my mobile with me on dangerous spying missions. Just in case.

eighteen

A DISEMBODIED HEAD

I positively swarm back up the rope, easily managing even the hardest part, which is getting a good enough foot grip on it so that I can grab onto the open skylight frame and boost myself up. The iron frame cuts into my fingers when I put my full weight on my hands. This would have been so much easier a few years ago, when I had the body of a little girl. But everything was easier when I was twelve. I flew on the bars so easily. Lifting my own body weight was nothing.

I push away the momentary flash of self-hate—I'm so fat, etc., etc.—and clamber out onto the roof. Squatting down, I lower the skylight back into place, propping it slightly open with the coil of rope, just in case I ever need to sneak in there again. And then I'm running across the roof, lowering myself down onto the fire escape, and picking my way down it to the top-floor window, in a tearing hurry to find Lizzie and confront her.

Only there's a bit of a hitch with that, because as my head comes round the corner of the window, scouting out to check that there's no one in the corridor, I freeze in horror. I'm looking directly into the beady eyes of Miss Newman, who is just coming round the corner of the corridor, heading toward the staircase.

Noooooooooo! I duck my head back again and flatten myself against the wall, praying to God that she didn't see me.

There's what feels like the longest silence ever in the history of the world. Then, over the sound of my heart trying to pound its way right through the wall of my chest, I hear a booming "*Oh, dear God in heaven!*" so deep that it sounds like a melancholy whale complaining about how miserable the world is.

I hardly dare to breathe.

"Maureen? What ees eet?" comes another voice.

This one is equally recognizable. It's Mamselle Fournier, the French teacher.

"Louise, the most *extraordinary* thing just happened. I thought I saw a disembodied head in that window!"

"*Mon Dieu!*" exclaims Mamselle Fournier.

I have to say that despite my panic at being discovered, I am also very creeped out by hearing teachers call each other by their first names. It's not that I don't know on some level that teachers have private lives and first names like everyone else. But I really don't want to think about it.

"Was eet *floating in the air?*" Mamselle Fournier asks. "Like a ghost?"

"No, no," Miss Newman's voice raises in pitch. "It was more . . . *fleeting*. Like a sudden vision."

"So eet was just zere for a moment?"

"Yes, that's right. Just a moment."

Mamselle Fournier, I think, clears her throat.

"Are you sure eet was a '*ead*? Per'aps eet was a *bird* zat you saw? Or a pigeon?"

There's a pause.

"I don't know," Miss Newman confesses. "I could have *sworn* it was a head . . . but maybe . . . "

"Maureen?" says Mamselle, " 'Ave you been feeling quite well? Do you per'aps 'ave a 'eadache?"

"Not really," Miss Newman intones. "But I think I feel one coming on . . . "

"'Ave you been per'aps under stress?"

"Not really. But *now* I feel *very stressed indeed*."

"Well, *naturellement* . . . eet ees very stressful to see 'eads that are not zere! Very stressful! I zink per'aps you should menzion zis to the school nurse, Maureen."

"Maybe it was one of the girls! Larking around!" Miss Newman booms, clearly not madly keen on this portrait of herself as an incipient loony two steps away from a strait-jacket and a padded cell.

I hear firm strides on the stone floor, and freak out. Someone is coming straight for the window. I cower on the fire escape, not daring to make a dash for it up onto the roof. They'd hear my feet on the iron steps.

I'm trapped. I am in so much trouble my head can't even get round the amount of trouble that I'm in. And then I hear a third voice. It's unmistakable, because it, too, has an accent.

An American one.

"Miss Newman! I just saw this *gigantic* squirrel!"

I can hear Miss Newman swing round. Nothing in this world, not even a mysterious disembodied head, will stop her from sinking her teeth into a girl who's breaking school rules.

"Taylor McGovern!" she says. "You are *completely* out of bounds!"

"I know, Miss Newman. I'm really sorry. I got completely turned around looking for the back staircase and now I'm, like, totally lost. But just now out of the window, I saw this, like, *humunguous* squirrel running along the fire escape! It really freaked me out! I didn't know you had, like, giant squirrels in England!"

Taylor has adopted a stereotyped American Valley Girl voice. It makes her sound brainless, like the kind of girl who really might get lost in the teachers' wing. Good acting, if Miss Newman doesn't spot it . . .

"A squeeerrel!" exclaims Mamselle. "Zat is ze answer, Maureen! Eet was a squeeerel zat you saw!"

"A *squirrel?*" Miss Newman says, skeptical. "Let me just have a look outside to make sure."

Oh no. I can hear her heading for the window again.

"Zere is no one out zere!" cries Mamselle, her high heels

190

clicking on the floor behind Miss Newman. "Look, ze window ees too 'igh to reach, you would 'ave to climb up zere!"

"I just want to have a quick look outside!" Miss Newman insists, and she's so close now that she sounds right next to me; any moment she'll see that the window's open a crack.

"Ohmigod, it's over here!" Taylor calls, sounding like she's farther away. "It's running down the fire escape—you can see it from the hall window! Wow, it's as big as a dog! A big dog!"

Okay, Taylor, I think, *don't overdo it . . .*

There's a clickety-clack of running heels, as presumably the teachers turn and hurry down the hall to where Taylor is standing.

"It just jumped into that tree," Taylor says, "can you see it?"

"I can see nozzing," Mamselle declares. "But Maureen, you realize now eet ees a squeerel you see? Zis girl, she sees it, too, and she sees it ees a beeg squeerel, nozzing else."

There's a long pause.

"Oh God, my hands are all filthy," Miss Newman booms gloomily.

"Of course zey are! Come downstairs, we weell go to see ze nurse, she weell give you somezing zat weell 'elp you to feel better. You, Taylor ees your name? Follow us, please. I weell show you 'ow to return to the main staircase."

The voices move away again, and I realize from the sounds that they're all going down the stairs. My legs have gone all wobbly. I actually feel them collapsing underneath me. I sink to my knees, taking deep breaths, dropping my head down to get the blood flowing back to it. I must have been there for at least five minutes, calming myself down. I could do with a dose of whatever the school nurse is currently doling out to Miss Newman.

And then a beautiful thought floods through me, icing on the cake. Every time Miss Newman picks on me in class from now on, all I need to do to cheer myself up is remember her desperately trying to prove to Mamselle Fournier that she isn't going mad, while Mamselle Fournier drags her off to the school nurse to stuff her full of maximum-strength tranquilizers.

I sigh in happiness. This is turning out to be a really good day.

But there's another mystery to solve now: how on earth did Taylor manage to turn up just in time to save my arse?

nineteen

THE CENTER OF THE MAZE

Taylor's waiting for me as soon as I step onto legally-permitted-for-students territory—the head of the staircase at the beginning of the central school wing. She's sitting on the big stone newel post, swinging her legs, looking like she could wait there all day if she needed to. She doesn't say anything, so I make the first move.

"Thanks," I say. "I owe you one."

"Yep, you sure do," Taylor says with confidence.

Wow, she's direct.

"Why are you even here?" I ask curiously.

Taylor leans toward me, darting a quick look around to make sure no one can overhear us.

"Well," she begins, "I went back to the classroom to get something from my desk, and Lizzie was in there having a one-girl pity party."

"Oh yeah, what was that about?"

She laughs. "You'll love this. She's scared of the trampoline in gym class. But she's even more scared of Miss Carter, so she won't ask her if she can be excused having to do it. What a total wimp, right?"

"That was *it?*" I can't help laughing, too. "All that big sobfest was about *gym class?*"

Can that be true, I wonder? Was Lizzie really crying about jumping on a trampoline, or were the tears about leaving that second note for me? I file this question away for later, when I'm alone. I have no intention of confiding everything in Taylor, even if she did just save me from imminent disaster.

"Uh-huh. So she told me, and I burst out laughing, which really wound her up."

That's what made Lizzie so angry. I remember her jumping up and shouting at Taylor.

"And then Meena came to see what was going on, and when Lizzie told her, Meena ticked me off for laughing at Lizzie," Taylor continues, "blah blah blah, more crying, hearts bleeding everywhere, and then I saw this flash of light in the window. I figured out straight away what it was—the sun reflecting off binoculars. Plus, it had to be coming from the opposite wing of the building. So I guessed it was you. I mean, you're the only person round here who's involved in any sort of mystery. And I thought there was something sketchy about that envelope stunt you pulled today, even if I couldn't figure out what it was."

I'm stunned into silence. Taylor's really, really good.

"And even if it wasn't you," she continues, "I wanted to know what was up with the whole binocular thing. So I sneaked into the teachers' wing to get closer to what was going on. And then I heard Miss Newman yelling about a head, and I knew she must have spotted you somehow. I figured you'd need some help. I wasn't sure what was going on, but I thought it'd be a good distraction to make up a story about a giant squirrel. Might buy you time to get away, or something." She looks a little embarrassed, which is no mean feat for Taylor. "After you didn't tell on me about climbing into your room, I thought I owed you something."

"You completely saved me," I admit.

She grins. "You're welcome."

I stare at her.

"How come you're so good at this?" I ask.

She actually goes a little pink. Taylor? Blushing? I don't believe it.

"I want to be a private investigator when I leave school," she says. "I practice a lot."

I can't help it, but I'm impressed. "Well, I'd say it's probably your ideal career."

"You could be my first client," Taylor says excitedly. "I could help you investigate! I know something's going on. It's all about that boy who died, right? Dan? Okay, I read all your press clippings, I admit it, but you already knew that, didn't you? Come on Scarlett, *please*. I'm going crazy with boredom here. This place *blows*. There's, like, nothing else going on but work work work and totally sucky PE classes. I'm bored out of my mind."

We look at each other for a long time in silence.

"I'm still really pissed off that you broke into my room and read my private stuff," I say.

Her eyes widen in protest.

"I just made up for that!" she exclaims. "By saving you! Come on, you know I did!"

"You can't just make bargains in your own head," I say, "like 'I did this for you, so now it's okay that I did that other thing that pissed you off.' It's my decision whether you made up for it, not yours."

This comes out a bit convoluted, so I'm very surprised when Taylor ducks her head and blushes once more.

"Yeah, my dad says I do that," she admits. "He gets really ticked off with me. I'm sorry."

For the first time, she seems genuinely contrite. I've managed to push exactly the right button.

"It's pretty lonely here if you don't fit in," Taylor adds eventually.

She looks nonchalant, and her words are a generalization, but I know how much it costs butch, self-reliant Taylor to make that kind of admission. I know because it would be just as hard for me to admit, even obliquely, how lonely I feel here at Wakefield Hall, surrounded by a school full of intellectual geniuses whose idea of a great Saturday night is to make hot cocoa and sit around translating Shakespeare sonnets into Latin. (I'm serious. That's what Meena and Susan do at the weekend.)

I weigh things up in my head. On the pro side, Taylor seems incredibly good at anything spying-related: she broke

196

into my room and went straight for the most important secret there was to find, not to mention that she was able to recognize the flash of the binoculars and get over to the teachers' wing in time to concoct a plan to save my bum. That makes her a really good ally. Cons: well, I was furious when I caught her in my room, going through my stuff. But she *did* make up for it by saving me just now, I decide. Without her, I'd have been toast.

And it *is* lonely here, particularly if you have a whacking great mystery to solve all by yourself.

"Okay," I say cautiously. "But not here. Come back to my place and I'll fill you in on a couple of things."

Intense excitement lights up Taylor's face, and she whoops and punches the air. But then, realizing she's showing weakness, she gets control of herself, reverting to her usual stone-cold, too-cool-to-show-emotion persona.

I grin. Taylor is the most macho girl I've ever met in my life. If I can trust her—and that's a big "if"—she'll make the most amazing ally.

And maybe I don't have that much choice in the matter. A girl who can shin up drainpipes and recognize the flash of binoculars catching the sun, who can make up a story on the spot to save someone else from being caught, well, put it this way: it feels a lot safer to have Taylor on my side than against me.

* * *

"So that's actually Versace?" I am saying, wide-eyed, as Lizzie and I stroll out of the cafeteria and onto the main terrace. Actually, my eyes are wide because I'm so bored I'm having to exaggerate, forcing the muscles to stay open, but Lizzie doesn't pick up anything unnatural about my expression. She's not exactly the Brain of Britain, I'm quickly coming to realize.

"Yeah!" Lizzie pats her handbag triumphantly. "It was in *Lucky* last month, and Lindsay Lohan was carrying one just like it, but in chocolate, on the cover of *Heat* two weeks ago." She pauses for thought. "Well, actually, her bodyguard was carrying it, because she was holding a coffee and a pack of cigarettes, so she'd given it to him to hold, or something, but anyway, she has one just like it!"

"That's so cool," I say.

The above sentence is carrying me through most of this conversation. It's the day after I saw Lizzie slip the note into my desk, and I've wasted no time in smarming up to her: I made sure I was just behind her in the cafeteria queue for lunch. Then, craftily, I said something about hoping they had salad today, because I was on a huge diet, and Lizzie immediately responded with the comment that if they served lasagne *one more time* she was going to completely *lose* it, because honestly sometimes she thought she put on weight just by *looking* at a tray of lasagne, which is just disgusting on *every* *level*, *wheat* and *cheese* and *red meat*, honestly, sometimes she thought the school was just trying to *fatten us up like pigs!* And then Lizzie started to do a running commentary on every single food choice in front of us with a rundown of its calorie, fat, and sugar content, and we found a table and sat down together, and Lizzie never stopped talking once, except to draw breath.

After that I've basically just been agreeing with everything she says, which seems to be working perfectly. Blimey, she can talk. I'm beginning to think Lizzie is as lonely as I am, though for a very different reason. She's a complete fish out of water here, with her elaborately tasseled bag, her highlighted hair, and the lip gloss she doggedly applies every half-hour in imitation of her heroines, even though no one here has the least appreciation for whether her lips are sticky and strawberry-scented.

Her main subjects of conversation are diets and fashion. It's a shame for Lizzie they don't offer an A Level in Celebrity Accessorizing, because she'd nail that exam with no revision necessary. In the hour I've spent with her, she's given detailed descriptions of the latest trends in Prada shoes, Stella McCartney belts, and, for all I know, Marc Jacobs bobby pins.

I couldn't quite recall the specifics, because I've been tuning out as much as possible, just nodding and smiling and murmuring "That's so cool" at regularly paced intervals. Gucci, Pucci, and Fiorucci have melted together in one fashion-obsessed rhyming blur. I'm as keen to look nice and trendy as the next girl, but Lizzie is up to her neck in the quicksand of celebrity lore and sinking fast. I can almost feel my brain melting into gray mush as I listen to her stream of consciousness.

At least now we're walking. After we finished our paltry lunch (there *was* salad, which was all Lizzie took, and I followed suit to ingratiate myself with her, and now I'm so hungry it feels as if my stomach's eating itself) we wandered outside. I was crossing my fingers that Lizzie wouldn't, at this stage, find anything suspicious in the fact that the girl into whose desk she slipped an anonymous note yesterday was suddenly hanging out with her today. But I'm now realizing that Lizzie has absolutely no one to talk to here about the things that really matter to her—which teenage celeb popstar owns which latest Louis Vuitton handbag—and she's so desperate for conversation with a like-minded person that she'll take it wherever she can get it.

I don't know what she's been doing up till now. Probably talking to the Lime Walk trees about Stella McCartney stilettos.

Lizzie is so busy rattling on that she doesn't notice that I'm subtly steering the direction we're taking. Past the girls playing clap ball and French Elastic, around the stand of weeping willow trees, up to the opening of the maze.

"So then I rang up the main branch," she's babbling, "the one in New Bond Street, and asked how long the waiting list was, and they said *five months.* Can you believe it? *Five months!* And I said, But it'll be completely *over* by then! I mean, Lindsey Lohan has it *now!*"

"Well, her bodyguard does," I mutter, unable to resist.

"Sorry?" Lizzie says, turning to me.

"Um, yeah!" I say. "I mean, who wants to wait five months for a handbag?"

"Well, *exactly*!" Lizzie agrees. "So I said, well, is there a different color? Because I don't have to have it *exactly* the same as Lindsay's. I mean, it's not about *copying* her or anything."

Luckily, she doesn't expect a response to this barefaced lie.

Just then she realizes the direction in which we've been walking.

"Are we going into the *maze*?" Lizzie asks nervously.

We've just arrived at the entrance. It's now or never. If I can get her in, we've done it. I take a deep breath and make my voice as casual, as light and breezy, as I possibly can.

"Yeah, I usually sit in the middle after lunch," I say.

"The *middle*? You know how to get to the *middle*?"

"Oh yes, it's really easy."

Lizzie stares at me. Her eyes are quite small, but she's carefully penciled and shadowed them till they look a lot bigger than they actually are. If she were at St. Tabby's, she'd be wearing a lot more makeup, but Wakefield Hall is really strict—you're not allowed to wear makeup till you're fifteen—and Lizzie's pushing the envelope with the amount of eyeliner she's wearing as it is.

Even with the makeup, though, Lizzie's eyes are tiny at the moment, because she's squinting them in confusion.

201

Then they open a bit, and she says, her forehead clearing of its frown, "Oh yeah! I forgot that you live here, sort of. I mean, that it's like your home."

I nod. "There's a trick to getting through the maze super-fast," I say, "like a shortcut. Here, I'll show you."

I step forward, through the entrance. The Wakefield Hall maze isn't the oldest one in England (that's Hampton Court) or the biggest (that's at Longleat, and I think it's made of sixteen thousand yew trees, i.e., it's massive) but it was planted over a hundred and fifty years ago, and the yews are ancient, tightly packed, and so intertwined by growing so close together that they're a wall as thick and strong as if it was made of stone. Most girls, I know, are scared to come into the maze: the hedges are so dense that it doesn't get a lot of sunlight, especially because it's shaded by the over-growing oaks that surround it. The little girls dare each other to go inside for five minutes, and usually come out trembling with fear.

But to me, it's just another part of my home. I remember my dad taking me in on his shoulders when I was really small. It's so tall that even sitting up there, on my six-foot dad, I couldn't see over the top of the hedges.

I always felt safe when I was with my dad. I know that, even though I don't remember much about him or my mum. They died when I was five, and the memories I have of them are all blurred at the edges, like old, fading photographs, where the dark is slowly moving in from the sides to obscure the picture.

But I know I always felt safe when he was around.

My dad showed me the shortcut the summer before they died. He was worried about me wandering inside and getting lost, and the shortcut is easy to remember: he made me repeat it till he knew I had it thoroughly memorized. Right, left, right, left, through the dead end, and right again. The dead end is a sort of hidden opening, which you can only find if you know it's there: you'd swear it was a solid cul-de-sac of hedge unless you went right up to it, and then you see the narrow chink to your right, just room enough for someone to wiggle through. Ted Barnes knows about it, because he's the one who prunes the maze—it's his job and he won't let anyone else do it.

And then I think about Jase Barnes, incredibly handsome Jase Barnes, with his golden eyes and butterscotch skin, and wonder whether, now Ted's getting older, he's letting Jase prune the maze hedge, and then I flash to a fantasy of it being Jase walking by my side now, instead of Lizzie, who's dutifully following me, still rabbiting on about celebrity handbags, and the thought sends butterflies through my stomach, which actually, though it sounds pretty and romantic, is actually quite an unsettling and dizzy-making sensation.

Jase Barnes. Kissing Jase Barnes, like I kissed Dan, feeling Jase Barnes's hands on me.

Jase Barnes, so tall and handsome, with those wide shoulders . . .

I shiver and push the thought of Jase firmly away from

me. I can't even think about him now. Still, this quest, this need to find out why Lizzie left me that note, is all about Jase Barnes, in a way; it's not only about what really killed Dan, it's also about whether I will ever be able to trust myself enough to kiss another boy ever again.

This quest is the single most important thing in my life.

"It's so *dark* in here," Lizzie's saying in a whiny voice.

I'm nipping through the maze so fast she's having to trot to keep up. She's like a Labrador, I realize, silly and trusting, ready to jump up and lick anyone who's being at all nice to her. I wonder how she got like this. And then I think about what happened to me to stop me being trusting. Lizzie's like a kid no one's ever truly been nasty to. She trots on blithely, as if the world were sugarcoated, like a child in the beginning of a fairy tale before she meets the monsters and the evil fairies and has to fight for her life.

I am very jealous of Lizzie.

"Is this really a *shortcut?*" she's whining.

Of course it isn't. I would never show Lizzie the shortcut. It's a family secret.

"Nearly there!" I say brightly.

And that's the truth. In a few more twists and turns, we emerge into the center of the maze, and Lizzie gasps in amazement and appreciation.

It's really pretty in here. The oak trees are trimmed so that on sunny days there's sunlight streaming down into the center of the maze, no overhanging branches to shadow the marble statue with the bench sculpted into its base, a statue that my great-great-great-grandfather (I think, I get confused by all those greats) had commissioned specially for this place. Then he planted all the yew trees around it, so they would grow to form the maze and conceal the statue.

The oak trees need cutting back, I notice: it's a bit dark in here, a bit overgrown. But that's perfect for my purpose today.

You can hide much better in the shadows.

I walk over to the bench and sit down, smiling at Lizzie. "Isn't it lovely?" I say in the same fake bright tone of voice. I pat the bench next to me. But instead of following and sitting down obediently, like a good little Labrador, Lizzie stands hesitantly in the entrance.

"It's so dark!" she complains. "And it feels damp! I don't like the damp."

"It isn't *damp*," I say crossly, "it's just a bit overgrown."

"Well, I don't like it." She's acting as if she were six years old rather than sixteen. "It's creepy. Can we go now?"

I brace myself to convince her to stay.

"Come on . . . ," I start, but that's as far as I get.

Lizzie turns to look behind her, at the opening in the hedge through which we just entered the center of the maze. And then a figure barrels into her out of nowhere and rugby-tackles her to the ground. They fall in a thrashing mess of tangled limbs and roll over till they come to rest almost at my feet.

"Taylor!" I yell, jumping up. "What on *earth* do you think you're doing?"

* * *

"I thought she was going to try to get away," Taylor says sullenly.

"Of course she wasn't going to get away!" I practically yell. "She's in the middle of the maze! Where would she go?"

"She looked like she was going to make a run for it," Taylor mutters.

"Ugh!" I shake my head in disbelief. Surely Taylor's seen enough of Lizzie's character to realize that she's too much of a scaredy-cat to seriously contemplate running through the maze on her own. Look at her—one little rugby tackle and a bit of rolling on the grass and she's crumpled up sobbing helplessly. "Lizzie? Can you sit up? I'll give you a hand."

Lizzie looks up tearfully and takes my proffered hand. I pull her up and we both sit down on the bench, as originally planned before Taylor went all ninja on her.

"I'm sorry about Taylor," I say, glaring at the girl in question. "She gets a bit carried away sometimes."

"She *hurt* me!" Lizzie wails.

"Yeah, she doesn't know her own strength."

"Hey, stop talking about me as if I was your tame gorilla!" Taylor snaps.

"Well, don't throw people around like you were starving and they were between you and the banana tree!" I snap back.

Lizzie looks terrified, as well she might.

"You two are really scaring me!" she moans.

"Well," I say to her, "all you have to do is tell us what we want to know and I'll take you straight out of here. Okay?"

Lizzie's expression is pretty much what Little Miss Muffet must have looked like when the spider sat down beside her.

"I don't know what you're talking about," she says feebly.

"Oh come on, Lizzie." I'm impatient now. "The note you left in my desk! You're not getting out of here till you tell me all about it."

Lizzie wells up like a fountain turned on full blast. "I can't tell you!"

I sigh, and look at Taylor, who's pantomiming sticking her finger down the back of her throat to indicate how nauseating she finds Lizzie's sobfest.

"Lizzie," I say, "you tell me or I'll tell my grandmother all about the note, okay? Your choice."

It's a totally empty threat, of course I won't tell my grandmother. But Lizzie doesn't know that. And she goes white at the thought of being hauled into the headmistress's study to be cross-examined.

"I know this wasn't your idea," I say, taking a guess.

But Taylor and I have talked this over, and neither of us believes that the note originated with Lizzie. She's such a wimp. It's hard to believe her generating something like this. My assumption is that she's acting on behalf of someone else . . . someone who isn't a pupil at Wakefield Hall. Luce? Alison? Is it far-fetched to think that, while they don't want to talk to me directly, they might have got Lizzie to leave me a note designed to make me feel better? It's not much of a theory, but I don't have a better one at the moment.

"Aaaaaaaaaah . . . " Lizzie's sobbing so hard I'm getting worried that her eyeballs are going to pop out under the pressure.

Taylor leans forward. She's clearly decided to up the threat level.

"Listen, you little crybaby—" she starts, in a voice so menacing that I get chills.

"Is everyone okay?" asks someone just around the corner of the maze.

The next moment he emerges. I stare at him, horrified. I might have fantasized about coming into the maze with Jase Barnes, but it didn't involve having two other girls present as well. And it certainly didn't involve him catching me in the middle of an interrogation.

THE HOTTEST GARDENER EVER

Jase is carrying a big pair of shears, and his T-shirt sleeves are rolled up to the caps of his shoulders, making his upper arms look bulgy with muscle. His faded old blue jeans hang loose on his lean hips, and there's the faint sheen of sweat on his cappuccino skin, his tight black curls a little damp with exertion.

If my grandmother had just entered the center of the maze wearing a bikini and a tiara, she couldn't have been more effective at getting our attention than Jase Barnes looking like the hottest gardener ever in his sweaty work clothes. We turn, stare at him and promptly freeze to the spot, as if we're playing a game of Musical Statues.

"Scarlett?" he says. "Are you okay? I was pruning the hedge, and I heard someone crying. I thought they might be lost in here."

His voice trails off as he takes in the scene. Suddenly I see the situation through Jase's eyes. One girl, slumped on the bench, crying her eyes out. Two girls, standing over her menacingly. Taylor and I must look like a pair of really nasty bullies.

And I *hate* bullies. How did I get myself into this? Because, although my motives are good, what we're doing is bullying Lizzie. No question about it.

I feel like a piece of dog poo.

Taylor and Lizzie flick their gaze in my direction, though they seem physically incapable of actually turning their heads away from Jase. I know exactly what they're thinking: this hunk of gorgeous boyhood, this slightly sweaty essence of handsomeness, actually *knows my name?* Knows me well enough to talk to me this familiarly? How lucky am *I?*

"Um, Lizzie was upset," I say weakly, "and we were trying to cheer her up."

"Doesn't seem to be working, does it?" Jase points out, and there's an edge to his voice now. He puts down the shears and comes over to the bench, kneeling down in front of Lizzie.

"You all right, love?" he asks gently.

Lizzie's ducked her head now and is rubbing at her face furiously. Finally, she lifts it to look at Jase, and Taylor and I involuntarily take a step back. Even Jase can't help jerking his head back reflexively. Lizzie looks like she's got hives. Her face is swollen and red and blotchy, and because of the rubbing, her eyeliner's all smudged, giving an extra Goth-y touch to the horror of her facial swelling.

"Um, you don't look good," he says with concern. "Anyone got a tissue?"

"I do." Lizzie whispers, and fumbles in the chartreuse abomination. She produces a pack of tissues and blows her nose. I'm amazed that she's got any fluid left in there at all—it sounded as if she'd cried it all out by now.

"That better?" Jase says.

Lizzie nods, her eyes now fixed on his golden ones. She looks more like a Labrador puppy now than ever.

I realize that I am horrendously jealous of Lizzie once again. How dare she be monopolizing Jase's attention like this? *I'm* the one he talks to, the one whose name he knows.

"Can you tell me what's wrong?" Jase asks, and he reaches out his hands to take hers.

My envy is so acute now I have to curl my toes till they hurt to stop me leaning forward and dragging the two of them apart. *I'm* the one whose hands Jase holds! *I* am! Not Lizzie!

Lizzie parts her lips, staring at him, and I realize with horror that she's about to talk. She's going to tell him everything. And when she does, it will all come out. Lizzie may not know whether I'm the Kiss of Death girl, but I'll have to explain it to him so he understands the whole picture, why Taylor and I were ganging up on her, and then he'll realize who I am and never want to come near me again, in case he drops dead because of kissing me, too.

"She's scared of doing trampoline!" Taylor blurts out.

Oh no, I think in panic, why did Taylor have to say that? It's the explanation Lizzie gave her of why she was crying in the classroom, but Lizzie surely must have been crying about something to do with leaving me the note. . . . Jase isn't going to believe this for a moment!

211

Jase turns his head to stare at Taylor.

"You *what?*"

"Yeah! She has to do it in gym class, and she hates it, but she's too scared to tell our coach she doesn't want to do it!" Taylor rattles out at high pitch.

Jase looks disbelievingly back at Lizzie.

"Is that really true?" he asks.

There's a long pause. Lizzie's hands are still in his, and she's showing no inclination of pulling them away. She gulps hard, still looking at him, and I know I need to get her attention *now*, or she'll break down and tell him everything.

"I was suggesting I could talk to my *grandmother* about it," I break in. "You know, she shouldn't have to get on a trampoline if she doesn't want to. People have accidents sometimes. On the springs. Um, it really does happen. So I thought, if I talked to my *grandmother*, she might change the rule that everyone has to do it."

Out of the corner of my eye, I see Taylor nodding in appreciation of the way I've gone along with her flash of inspiration. The only thing that mattered in my little speech was emphasizing my close connection to the headmistress—i.e., reminding Lizzie of my threat to tell my grandmother about the note unless she came clean about it to us.

And it seems to have worked. Lizzie gulps again, and says to Jase in such a small voice it's almost a whisper:

"I *am* scared of the trampoline. I always think I'm going to fall. It's really . . . bouncy."

Taylor does her best to stifle a snort of laughter, but Jase catches it.

"Hey, she's scared!" he says angrily to Taylor. "You should respect that. Everyone's scared of something." And then to Lizzie he adds dubiously, "Is that really it? Is that really why you were crying so hard you sounded like you were going to burst a blood vessel?"

Jase is no fool. He can tell there's more to this than meets the eye. I hold my breath, but Lizzie nods her head, her eyes widening.

"There are these springs! On the edge of the trampoline!" she says. "I'm always scared I'm going to land on them and hurt myself! They look really dangerous, I can't *believe* they actually make us jump near them! I told my dad but he said he was sure the school knew best, and he's so busy all the time anyway, but I really hate doing it and I'm sure Miss Carter makes me do it on purpose because she's mean like that."

My God, it's true. Lizzie really is scared of the trampoline. Taylor and I exchange glances of disbelief. And Jase has realized by now that once Lizzie gets started babbling, she won't stop of her own accord, He lets her hands go (about time, too!) and stands up.

"And you two were teasing her about it, were you?" he says to me and Taylor.

"We were trying to help," I lie. "We just weren't doing a very good job of it."

"You can say that again," he says dryly, and when his eyes meet mine there's none of the warmth I've come to expect from him. "I'll get going, then. That hedge isn't going to clip itself, more's the pity."

He picks up his shears from the grass beside the bench.

"You sure you're going to be okay?" he asks Lizzie. "Do you want me to walk you out?"

He doesn't trust us. Me and Taylor. He doesn't trust us to take care of a sobbing, upset girl. And the worst part is that he's absolutely right.

Lizzie looks up, and her face illuminates for a moment with hope, hope that she'll be able to leave the maze now, with Jase as her protector, save herself from anymore blackmail by me and Taylor. And then she catches sight of me, and I shake my head, the tiniest of motions—I hope to God Jase didn't see it—but enough to convey to her that there's no easy escape for her, no flight with Prince Charming. She has to stay here and face the music, that's what the shake of my head says, or I'll go straight to my grandmother.

"No, I'm fine," she mutters. "Thanks. I'll stay here."

Jase shrugs, a big circling of his muscular shoulders that comprehensively conveys his wish to put this whole messy scene behind him and get on with his work. He looks straight at me for a second as he turns to exit through the gap in the hedge, but it's a cold, direct stare, nothing friendly about it at all. And then he's gone.

I want to burst into tears. I want to run after him and throw myself into his arms and confess everything. But that would be ridiculous. I barely know him. And telling him wouldn't solve anything. I had to make a choice, and that's what I did: look good in front of Jase, or push forward on finding out what happened to Dan. And I chose the latter. What I need to focus on is right here in front of me: Lizzie, who has a piece of the puzzle in her fluffy little brain. Lizzie, whose information will get me one step closer to solving the mystery of Dan's death.

I tell myself it's better this way. It's better that Jase thinks I'm a bully and a bitch. Because if he does, he'll stay away from me, and I won't have to deal with my attraction for him while Dan's death is unresolved. I won't be tempted to kiss him and have to push him away, afraid that my weird curse will somehow transmit itself to him.

I tell myself all that, but it doesn't help at all. Jase's eyes, always so warm and glowing and golden when they look at me, were like frozen metal just now, icy and hard. I hate that he looked at me like that. Hate it.

I gulp. Taylor's looking at me, frowning, her straight dark brows drawn together over her slanting green eyes. It's as if she screamed, "Pull yourself together, Scarlett!"

I nod at her. Then Taylor and I both look at Lizzie. We don't even need to speak. Lizzie is broken by now, broken by having cried so hard, having had several opportunities to tell Jase the truth and taken none of them, having been offered passage to safety through the maze by him and rejected it. I know that one good hard menacing stare from both of us will be more than enough to make her give up her secret.

And so it proves.

Twenty-one

BAD COP/BAD COP

I told Lizzie to start from the beginning. I realize now that may have been a mistake. I'm just surprised she didn't start by recounting her birth. Blimey, this girl likes the sound of her own voice.

"I'm really in debt," Lizzie says, winding a tissue through her fingers. "I keep thinking that if I have the latest bag or whatever, they'll let me be friends with them. And it does sort of work. I mean, they ask me to parties sometimes, and if I'm in the same club they'll let me sit with them if I buy lots of drinks. But Dad's actually quite strict about my credit card, he monitors it online and he shouts at me if I go over a grand, which is *nothing*, actually, I can't *believe* he's that fussy when he's a multimillionaire, you know?"

Lizzie's incapable of holding more than one thought in her head at any one time: from her indignant tone, I can tell that she's so resentful at her father's injustice that she's temporarily forgotten to be frightened of me and Taylor. She starts shredding the tissue she's holding, ripping it up angrily. Bits of white floaty paper drift off in the breeze and fall to the grass below the bench.

"Anyway, I'm really skint after buying this bag." She looks dolefully at the ghastly chartreuse thing with its dripping straps and buckles and shiny dangling bits. "I wanted to go out this weekend, but I can't, because I haven't got a *penny*, and then she offered me all this money if I'd just leave a note for you, Scarlett." Lizzie looks up at me, her eyes still swollen, but with a genuinely imploring expression that makes me think she's telling the truth here. "She swore it wasn't anything bad, just that she didn't want you to know it came from her."

"Why not?" Taylor asks.

"I don't know, she didn't tell me and I didn't ask. I mean, it was *two hundred and fifty pounds*! Just for leaving you a note! And then the first one you had a pen leak on, so I had to go and get another one from her, which was really hard to organize because I had to be back by curfew and she made this huge fuss about coming out on the tube to meet me. *Wait . . .* "

The penny dropped. Lizzie stares at both of us in shock.

"You didn't have an ink leak, did you?" Lizzie says, her voice rising. "It was all a *setup*. You did that *deliberately* so I'd have to get another note and you could watch me put it in the desk and I *still* don't know how you saw me! Unless Meena saw me, but when I came out of the room she was halfway down the corridor. Did you have a video or something in there?"

Taylor and I just look back at her, stone-faced, not giving anything away.

She sighs. It'd be a sob if she had any tears left. As it is, she just looks down at the shredded tissue on the grass, and sighs again.

"No one ever tells me *anything*," Lizzie complains. "That note was sealed up, so I couldn't see what it was, and now you won't tell me how you knew it was me! It's so unfair."

"Life sucks, Lizzie," Taylor says nastily. "Deal with it."

I expect now I should be good cop, to Taylor's bad, but I haven't got the energy to pretend to be nice. This last half hour has been really draining. I decide that we'll go for bad cop/bad cop instead. It'll be quicker.

I fix Lizzie with a hard stare, and say:

"What's her name, Lizzie? The girl who paid you to slip me that note?"

Lizzie starts shredding another tissue.

"I promised I wouldn't tell," she whines. "And she was going to let me go clubbing with them on Saturday and not make me pay for everything, like they usually do . . ."

Taylor walks over to the bench, kneels down in front of Lizzie, and grabs her shoulders. Blimey. Taylor must look enormous from that angle, her jaw jutting forward, her arms swelling under her T-shirt. Her hands are really strong, too, and calloused from all the rope climbing. Lizzie visibly wilts in her grasp.

"You're out of time," Taylor says. "Give us the name. Now."

219

Double-blimey. Taylor is *fantastic* at being bad cop. I just hope she never turns on me.

Lizzie droops as if she has no backbone at all, as if she's just made of jelly. Her head hanging, she stares down at the grass, and whispers a name, so softly that I don't catch it.

"What did she say?" I demand.

My heart's pounding. We're getting closer to finding out at least part of this mystery, the real truth of what happened that night, the answer to why Dan died.

Taylor lets go of Lizzie, who flops onto the bench.

"Nadia," Taylor tells me. "She said Nadia."

Twenty-Two

OPERATION OBNOXIOUS AMERICAN

It was really hard to wait till the weekend to stake out Nadia's block of flats. But there was no way we could get into town long enough to do anything during the week, what with the Wakefield Hall seven p.m. dinner curfew, we'd barely get to Knightsbridge before we'd have to turn around and come home again. On the weekends, we're free from noon on Saturday onward, as long as we're home by seven for dinner, of course. That's like an alternative religion for my grandmother—dinner at seven. And Sundays we can get away all day till dinner, as long as we present a plausible schedule of what we're doing to our housemistress, and have at least one other girl to go out with.

(Bad luck on loners, that rule, I always think. I mean, what a way to make you feel even worse if you don't have a friend or two to go out with on the weekends.)

We told our housemistresses (or, in my case, Aunt Gwen) that we wanted to go and explore London parks. Not a complete lie. Aunt Gwen, honestly, wouldn't have cared less if I'd said I wanted to go and explore London crack dens; but Taylor's housemistress, Mamselle Fournier, apparently clapped her hands and said what a charming idea that was. Bless Mamselle Fournier. I've had an incredibly soft spot for her ever since the whole incident in the corridor with the disembodied head and her persuading Miss Newman that she might be insane.

So here we are, sitting with our backs against trees, curled up in the roots, looking for all the world like two teenagers hanging out in Hyde Park on a Sunday afternoon with nothing better to do with our lives.

"He'll never talk to me again," I say, picking a blade of grass and twisting it between my fingers, tighter and tighter, till it darkens and gets soggy with moisture. I drop it to the ground, where it joins a pile of other blades of grass, equally tortured and discarded.

"Come on, Scarlett. It's only been a few days," Taylor says.

"But he thinks I'm a bully now. I'm sure he's avoiding me."

"Hey, you can't know that!"

"I just think I'd have seen him around before now."

"He might have had a couple of days off!"

I sigh. "No, he's avoiding me, I'm sure of it. I really think he liked me a bit."

"Sure he did. You could tell he liked you when he came into the maze."

"Oh yeah?" I perk up despite my gloom. "How?"

"The way he looked at you," Taylor says. "It was totally obvious."

"But now he thinks I'm a mean girl—"

"When this is all over, you can go and tell him everything," Taylor says firmly. "It'll make an amazing story. And then he'll, like, cover your face with burning kisses."

"He'll *what?*"

She grins.

It's in this P.G. Wodehouse book I'm reading to learn how to be more English. The hero just covered his girlfriend's face with burning kisses." She points to the book lying on the grass beside her. "Hey, nothing's happened with the stakeout while you've been boring me to death going on about that Jase guy, has it?"

I shake my head, my gaze fixed on Nadia's building, across the wide road that's Knightsbridge.

"No one in or out. I've been keeping an eye on it."

"Maybe Nadia's away for the weekend," Taylor comments.

It's the first time either of us have mentioned that possibility, though it's been on our minds ever since we got here. It's so frustrating. I scrabbled up from the depths of my memory the information that Nadia's parents were art dealers, and finding their gallery's phone number was easy enough. A call to the super-posh receptionist ascertained the information that they were "away on an acquisitions trip" till the end of next week. And the magic of the Internet also informed us that Nadia's brother Olivier is at Durham University, which is far enough away from London that we

223

could cross our fingers and assume he wouldn't be back for weekends much.

Which leaves Nadia. And the thought that she might have left for the weekend before we got here yesterday afternoon, and that we'll be sitting here all day Sunday, with the flat empty, just to watch her roll home sometime this evening, is so annoying that we've been deliberately avoiding expressing it to each other.

Taylor takes out her mobile and dials a number.

"I'm calling the flat again," she says, "just in case." She pauses, listening to the rings. "Ugh," she says crossly. "Answerphone again."

The trouble is, the fact that Nadia isn't picking up the phone doesn't mean she isn't there. All her friends would ring her on her mobile. So she probably wouldn't bother to get the house phone, assuming it would just be messages for her parents.

A few magazines lie scattered around us, which we've been thumbing through, but only with half an eye in my case, as I'm the one who knows what Nadia looks like, and I have to keep staring in the direction of that impressive glass entrance. Knightsbridge is wide enough to have four lanes of traffic, and I know Nadia won't bother to glance all the way across it over the low wall into the park, let alone have any interest in a pair of averagely dressed girls who can't remotely compete with her in any glamour or fashion stakes.

A black cab pulls up outside the building. There's someone in it, but they don't get out. It just sits there, idling its engine. After a minute or so, the doorman comes out and walks over to the big glass sliding entrance doors to see if the person in the cab needs anything, but the driver waves him away and he goes back inside. And then, a minute or so later—

"Oh my God!" I squeal.

"Keep it down," Taylor hisses. "Is it her?"

I've grabbed a magazine and am holding it up to obscure most of my face. It's Nadia, dressed in jeans and a tight sweater with a slit neck that shows her thin tanned shoulders. Her wrists are heavy with gold bangles. She exits the building and walks slowly toward the cab, waving at its occupant, throwing her head back to show off how shiny her hair is, extracting the maximum theatricality from this simple crossing of the pavement.

"Yeah, it's Nadia. And I think that's Plum in the cab," I inform Taylor, squinting to see through the tinted windows of the taxi.

"I can't believe she's the same age as us," Taylor says, gawking at Nadia's glamour.

"Aunt Gwen says Middle Eastern girls age faster," I say.

"Your aunt Gwen's an evil old hag," Taylor says. "I should know, I have her for geography."

"Nadia *is* really gorgeous," I say as Nadia bends to scoot her skinny frame into the cab.

Taylor sniffs. "It's all makeup. She probably looks like the back of a train in the mornings."

I crack up. "Taylor, it's a *bus*, not a train. You look like the back of a *bus* if you're ugly."

225

"Stupid English expressions," Taylor says sulkily. "There are millions of them, and they're all stupid."

The cab's pulled away.

"They'll be off to a really late lunch on the King's Road." I'm guessing, but I've probably got it more or less right. God knows I've heard them all banging on about what they did at the weekend thousands of times when I was still at St. Tabby's. "And then shopping in Sloane Street. We've got hours."

"Hopefully you won't need hours," Taylor says, standing up. "Ouch, my foot's gone to sleep." She shakes her trainer about. "Okay, let's get Operation Obnoxious American under way."

I jump up, too.

"Ready to be obnoxious?" I ask.

"Jesus, after all this waiting? You kidding? I am *totally* ready!" Taylor says, with an ominous gleam in her eye.

And then she looks at me long and hard.

"*You* ready?" she asks me.

I nod. I don't trust my voice just at this moment.

Taylor's task, though showy, has no danger involved. I'm the one who has the scary mission to complete.

Which I am trying very hard not to panic about.

*   *   *

"*Owww! Owww!* My *foot!* What the hell did I *trip* on? Owww!"

Taylor is eerily believable. If I didn't know this was all a setup, I'd absolutely think, like everyone else stopping to stare at her, that she'd just tripped on the carpet outside Nadia's block of flats, fallen, and done something nasty to her foot.

She's writhing around and grabbing it. No one's going up to her, at least not yet: she's making such a racket that the more repressed Brits are embarrassed by the noise. It's not that they don't want to help, it's that they're afraid that approaching her will inevitably draw them into the Scene she's making, and one thing English people are really scared of is Being Involved in a Public Scene. It's very shameful in our culture.

But there's a very good reason why Taylor is shouting the place down . . .

"Owww! It really hurts! Can I get some help here, please?" she yells in the direction of the glass doors.

The doorman has got to have seen Taylor lying there. He's probably hoping she'll eventually get up and walk away without involving him and his building in anything.

Taylor writhes on the carpet. "I think my ankle's twisted!" she yells. "I am so suing this building—that carpet's a total health risk! Who the hell puts *carpet* on a sidewalk, anyway?"

"Are you all right?" a young man says, stopping in front of her. He's wheeling a bike and wearing exercise gear.

"No, I'm not! I caught my foot on that carpet and now I think I've twisted my ankle!" she replies loudly.

"Oh crumbs," he says, "what a bore."

To my great amusement, Taylor actually stops wailing and writhing for a split second out of sheer surprise at this superb example of British understatement. She goggles at him as if he were in a freak show before recovering herself and saying pointedly: "Yeah, it hurts like hell!"

"Well, let me have a quick look," he says, propping the bike up against the building and coming to kneel beside her. "I'm a medical student, actually. Not quite as good as a proper doctor. But I think I should be able to look at an ankle."

Noooooooooo! I yell inside my head. If he gets his hands on her ankle, he'll see that she's completely fine, help her up, our entire plan will be ruined—

Taylor is panicking as well, as the same thought hits her.

"Uh, I'm not sure you should do that," Taylor says feebly, "because, of, um, medical insurance . . . liability . . . "

But just as the young man is reaching out to her allegedly twisted ankle, a third voice breaks in.

"You can't leave that bicycle against this building, young man!" it says reprovingly. "I'm going to have to ask you to move it at once."

Taylor and the medical student both turn to look. It's the doorman. Not the one who was on duty that fateful Saturday night of the party, a much older one, with a forbidding scowl. The medical student looks nervous. Taylor, however, rises magnificently to the occasion.

"I'm sorry, buddy, *what* did you say?" she asks angrily.

"This nice guy is trying to *help* me after I fell over and probably *broke* something on your stupid carpet, and you don't even bother to come out and check if I'm okay? Oh no, all you care about is a damn bike! If I've hurt myself, my mom will sue your asses from here to L.A. and back, believe me, and the fact that you didn't even bother to come out and see if I was okay will look really bad in court!"

"Um, steady on," the young man says uncomfortably to Taylor. "I don't actually mind moving my bike."

"You can both help me in right now so I can sit down inside instead of lying on some dumb *carpet on the sidewalk*, and this doctor guy can see if my ankle's okay!" Taylor continues, barely registering his interruption. "Or otherwise *you*"—she points at the doorman—"will be on the business end of a big fat lawsuit! My mom just *loves* to sue people!"

Blimey, I think, who is Taylor channeling? This isn't her at all, and she's doing it so well! The doorman starts to say something, but then he catches Taylor's eye and thinks better of it, I can tell.

"Let's get you into the lobby, then, miss," he says, coming over to where she's lying. "And perhaps after that the young gentleman wouldn't mind taking his bicycle round to the service entrance."

The medical student says something, and they both start helping Taylor up, but I barely catch this, as I am now in motion, sneaking along the pavement, close to the wall, moving fast and confidently, hitting the center of the gray doormat, which triggers the opening of the glass doors. Just as they start to open, which might catch the doorman's attention, Taylor, who's been keeping an eye on my progress, lets out a big "Owwww!" of pain and sags heavily against the doorman, so that his entire attention goes into not dropping her.

I'm in. My trainers make no noise at all on the marble floor as I sprint across it. This is one of the most dangerous bits of all, because I don't know where I'm going. I dart my head frantically from side to side, looking for what I know has to be around here somewhere. . . . Keep going, Scarlett, keep looking. . . . It's not behind the doorman's big desk, but it must be nearby, surely, because he'd need to get to it on a regular basis. I'm past the desk and scouring the wall with my eyes—a door! Yes! I dash toward it and pull it open. A second later and I'm inside—and not a second too soon, because I can already hear voices in the lobby. Taylor's is raised as loud as she can to warn me of their presence.

I look around me. I'm in a corridor—concrete floor, steel-gray walls, bright fluorescent lights running overhead—a stark contrast to the discreetly lit dark wood and marble of the lobby I've just come through. This is most definitely the servants' area of the building. Good. I move down the corridor listening intently in case there's anyone around, but the only noise I hear is my own breathing . . . and my sharply indrawn gasp of excitement as I round a corner and come face to face with what I'm looking for.

Three small lifts, set into the wall at waist-height. Each one of them with a sign over the top, reading:

Penthouse A, B, or C. I press the call button for C, and it opens immediately.

Oh God. I bend down and look inside. I'll fit, but it's going to be a tight squeeze.

I take a deep breath and brace myself. I knew what I was in for. I can't back out now.

I have to do this.

Before I can think it over anymore, I climb awkwardly into the lift. It's about the size of a kennel—for a big dog, thank God, a Doberman's kennel rather than a Chihuahua's. Still, it rocks beneath my weight. I have to wiggle round once I'm inside, so my upper body is at the front, and that makes it rock even more. I'm curled up tight, my trainers crammed against the far wall, and I reach out with one hand to press the button on the outside wall to start the lift moving, knowing that when I do, the doors will close, and I'll be shut inside this small airless space. It's the scariest thing I've had to do in my life.

I press the button and scoot my hand back inside as quickly as I can. The doors close. And the lift wobbles as the mechanism starts to engage. The floor I'm lying on jolts and rocks and starts to move upward, agonizingly slowly, so slowly that it feels it could jam and stop dead at any moment, trapping me in here.

It's pitch-black. I'm already getting a cramp, and I'm absolutely terrified. I close my eyes tight and say every prayer I know.

Twenty-Three

WHAT NADIA SAW

I have Taylor to blame for all of this. It was Taylor who had
the brilliant idea of looking up the details of the Farouk
penthouse online, so we could see if there might be any way
to sneak in. She found a big article in a glossy magazine
about the building, which apparently was new just a few
years ago, and in the gush of purple prose about its famous
architect and interior designer, we learned more about how
the very rich live than I really wanted to know. All the
penthouse apartments have saunas and wet rooms and built-
in climatized closets for fur storage and temperature-
controlled wine rooms. They also have service lifts, so that
when a delivery arrives downstairs with the doorman, no
one in Penthouse A, B, or C has to do anything as vulgar as
go downstairs to collect it (just imagine!). Instead, the doorman signs for it, rings upstairs to make sure someone's in to
receive it, and then puts it in the appropriate lift.

"Wow," Taylor had said, reading that aloud. "You could

order Chinese food and it would arrive *in your apartment*, like the restaurant was in your *basement*. How cool is *that?*"

For security reasons, the lifts aren't full-size, the article explained. From my perspective, they aren't even half-size. As the Penthouse C lift slowly judders and rattles its way up the shaft, I am packed in tighter than cartons of Chinese delivery food under a delivery guy's moped seat. My stomach is so squashed into my knees that I'm beginning to feel queasy. My face is pressed into the metal floor of the lift, which is really cold. And one of my feet is torqued at an odd angle, which is beginning to hurt.

It's stopped! My heart jolts as hard as the lift coming to a halt. I actually squeeze my eyes shut, so scared that I'm stuck in the lift shaft and Taylor will have to send in the troops to rescue me and we will both be in the worst trouble in the world.

The doors aren't opening. And it's not just my panic that's stretching time out infinitely, making the couple of seconds before they slide open seem like an eternity. Oh no. They're really not opening. And there's no thin strip of light between them that would show that we've reached Penthouse C, which would at least mean that I could try to force them open and climb out.

Oh God. I feel nausea rising up my esophagus. Acid bites at the back of my mouth. If I have to ring Taylor, this entire mission will be aborted . . . they'll have to get the Fire Brigade in to save me . . . Nadia will hear about it and she'll tell everyone at St. Tabby's, the humiliation will be worse than anything I've been through before, even Dan's death wasn't humiliating, because he *wanted* to kiss me, but *this*, well, I might as well just kill myself now.

It occurs to me that by the time the Fire Brigade or the lift engineers come that problem may well be solved. I will probably have run out of oxygen by then anyway. They'll have to drag my corpse out of the lift.

This idea is not as comforting as my brief fantasies of suicide might have made it seem. I thrash around frantically, trying to get to my mobile phone. But guess what? I am wedged so tightly into this dog-kennel of a lift that I can't get to my phone. I can feel its outline in my jeans pocket, but my arms are sandwiched between my legs and the walls, squashed in like a sausage in its casing, and I can hardly get any movement in them, let alone extract one and reach into my pocket. The phone is right there. It's actually digging uncomfortably into my thigh. But it might as well be on the moon for all the use it is to me.

I stop thrashing around, as that's making the lift rock precipitously and I'm scared I might break the cable and send it crashing to the ground floor. The acid in my throat is making me retch a little. I'm more frightened than I've ever been before in my life. And with horror, I realize something that hadn't occurred to me before.

I weigh too much for this lift. It's all my own fault. I am so fat that I have managed to jam this lift between floors. Oh God. What fun Plum and Nadia and Venetia and Sophie will have with this. I can't bear it. I physically can't bear it. My foot, which is twisted under me, is starting to hurt really badly now. I'm scared my entire body is going into spasm.

And then, suddenly, the lift jerks under me, like a horse that's finally decided to start walking again. I catch my breath, unsure if this is good or bad. But how could it be bad, how could movement be bad—even if we're going down again, at least I'm going *somewhere* there might be fresh air, which has to be better than this.

The lift sighs, clanks, gathers itself up, and starts rising again. My face presses harder into the metal floor as if it's coming up to squash me. I don't care. I don't care about anything but getting out of this bloody contraption. I am so grateful I could cry.

It stops again. I realize I'm still holding my breath. The doors ping open. Daylight floods in. I hear a weird yelping noise and realize that's me, letting out my breath on a hysterical sob of relief. I'm really glad no one else was around to hear that.

Ironically, it takes ages to untwist my pretzeled body and crawl out of the lift, and the doors keep trying to shut on different bits of me. But finally, I've clambered out and onto a granite shelf, which seems more than capable of bearing my weight. I sit there, looking around, getting my bearings, and firing off a quick text to Taylor so she knows I made it in okay and not to stage an emergency lift extraction on my behalf.

This place is even more impressive in the daytime. I'm

in the main hallway, and there's a big skylight above it which daylight pours down through its sheer sheet of glass, showing how shiny and spotless and gleaming every surface here is. Marble floors, granite shelves, walls painted faux-tortoiseshell, waist-high vases filled with exotic flowers. Their florist bill alone must be gigantic.

I jump down from the shelf and stroll into the living room, which I remember from the party. It looks like a film set. I can't believe people actually live here. The mirrored bar glitters with reflected sunlight bouncing off the faceted bottles and glasses, the leather sofas are arranged at perfect right angles to each other. There's nothing out of place here, not a newspaper thrown on the floor or a mug with coffee dregs standing on one of the many smoky-glass coffee tables.

Through the French doors I can see the terrace, and if I went up to them I could see the exact spot where Dan died. But I don't. It would be too much of a temptation to go outside, and I'm sure I can't, as the doors must be alarmed. Besides, I need to focus on what I'm doing, searching for anything that might help me work out why Nadia left me that note. If I start remembering that night right now, back in the place where it all happened, I know I'll start crying, and I mustn't do that. I mustn't. For all I know, Nadia might be back really soon. I didn't go through that terrifying ride in the lift just to get caught here by Nadia.

So I turn my back on the French doors and the terrace, setting my teeth against the temptation, and begin to make a circuit of the apartment, looking for Nadia's room. In the process, I learn something about myself: I am a horrible snoop. I want to look in *everything*, every single drawer and cupboard, open every door to see what's behind it. I am massively curious about how these people live, what they own, what their secrets are. I keep reminding myself that only Nadia is my business, but it's really hard to keep going through this lavishness without gawking at everything in sight.

The wet room and sauna are particularly impressive.

I don't know what I was imagining that Nadia's room would be like. I don't even realize it's hers at first. I mean, she just left it to go out to brunch, she's the only person in residence here, with no one to shout at her for not picking up her clothes from the floor, and yet her room is so tidy and spotless that at first I actually assume it's yet another spare bedroom. It's done in pale greens and even paler yellows and it looks incredibly elegant, like a guest room in a magazine, with everything matching and perfectly in place. The silk coverlet is embroidered with a pattern of white bamboo, and the bed is piled high with white and pale gold silk pillows that look pretty but must be really slippery to sit on or put behind your head if you want to curl up in bed. The light green carpet is so thick and plushy you could sleep on it. There's an ensuite bathroom all in pale yellow. It's gorgeous. It's just weird that it feels like no one actually lives here. I only realize it's Nadia's room when I open one of the wall-full of built-in cupboards and recognize her clothes hanging there. My God. She has an entire cupboard just for her jeans. I goggle at it for a long time in utter and complete jealousy.

Then I pull myself together and get to the task at hand: searching through her stuff. I don't know what I'm looking for, or even if there's anything to find. But Taylor and I decided that this had to be the first step. We didn't think that confronting Nadia would have any results at all: she'd just deny everything and say Lizzie is a delusional idiot, which, frankly, would be hard to counter. We need some evidence, something concrete.

There's a laptop on the built-in desk, open and humming quietly to itself, but I leave that as a last resort. When I write down private things, I don't put them on my computer. Computers can crash, or be nicked. People can hack into them and copy all your private stuff in five minutes and print out tons of copies for everyone else to laugh over. It happened to a girl at St. Tabby's a few years above us—someone worked out her password, accessed her diary, and put pages from it in everyone's pigeonholes, all about her secret crushes and how much she ate every day. After that, I'd never trust my private stuff to a computer, and I doubt any St. Tabby's girl would either.

It takes me fifteen minutes to find it. It isn't under the mattress. I didn't think there'd be anything there, because in a place this smart, the maid must be changing the sheets and turning the mattress on a regular basis, so that wouldn't be a safe place to hide anything. It's on the bookshelf, which is pretty clever of her. Like in "The Purloined Letter," where

239

the best place to hide something is in plain view, in a really obvious place, so no one would even think it was being hidden at all. It's in a row of books with similar spines, brightly colored hardbacks, and she's even gone so far as to write something on the spine, so at first or second glance it just looks like one of many, something your eye would skim over in passing. Nothing that would make you think: oh, that looks like a private diary! and pull it off the shelf for a good old snoop.

It's a really nice notebook, the size of a hardback book, covered in yellow and pink matte paper that feels very heavy and expensive. I sit down on the floor (the bed's so perfectly made I'm worried about creasing the silk coverlet, I don't think I could ever get it that smooth again, and I mustn't leave any signs of my presence here) and start thumbing through the pages.

The first words that catch my eye are the ones that started this whole thing:

"It wasn't your fault."

I read on, my whole attention riveted to the page.

I sit and look at those words for a long time. I want to write more, I really do.
But I'm scared.

I rip through the pages, speed-reading now.

The lesson is not that it's hard to keep a secret.
The lesson is that it's impossible to keep a secret.
This is too much for me to hold. I feels as if I'm going to explode with it. My head actually hurts with the effort of not telling anyone what I saw.

Okay, I take a deep breath and stop for a second. If Nadia saw something, she'll have written it earlier than this . . . earlier than her endless debates with herself about whether she should try to get me the information or not.

I flick back, and back, and back, looking for my name and Dan's.

Which aren't hard to find.

Scarlett came to school today to pick up her stuff. We had a go at her by her locker. She grabbed Plum and pushed her. I couldn't believe it. Plum was actually scared, you could tell. Ever since she got her chin reduced, she's been terrified of anything happening to her face.

I told Sophia I felt sorry for Scarlett. Big mistake. I can't believe I was that stupid. Plum owns Sophia. She just stared at me and said:

"But Scarlett got off with Dan, and Plum liked him! You don't do that! I mean, everyone knew Plum liked Dan!"

God, she's like a little Plum-bot—press a button in her back and Plum's voice comes out . . .

I can't help giggling at this. Plum-bot's pretty good.

But I'm a Plum-bot, too. We all are. I really fancied Dan and I would never have made a move, never, because of what Plum would have done to me. I'm as pathetic as Sophia.

Yes, you are, I think smugly.

And look at Scarlett! She's no better! She gave me this really stuck-up look when we were all having a go at her, but she dropped those two frumpy friends of hers like a shot when I invited her to my party! And then she turned up dressed just like us, not in that crappy exercise stuff she usually wears. Desperate to fit in. She's just as pathetic as we are!

Alison and Luce. She's right. I betrayed them. I feel so guilty it's like a big lump in my throat just thinking about them.

Nadia and I are the same. Or at least, we share something. The need to be liked and wanted, to be part of a cool group, to feel admired. And the moral weakness that means we'll make compromises, sacrifice things, to fit in. Alison and Luce, for me. And Nadia: well, you don't stay a slim-as-a-wand Plum-bot by eating nice nourishing healthy meals three times a day.

I flick back through the pages. Looking for my name.

Simon's got this huge crush on that girl Scarlett in our year. He spotted her sitting on a bench after school with those two ugly friends of hers. I don't know why she even caught his eye—they always look so shitty. Pink and shiny and dressed in really unflattering exercise clothes. It must be her tits. God, I'd love to have tits. Maybe I can talk Mother into paying for them. Venetia wants a boob job, too. We could go together.

Anyway, Simon keeps asking questions about Scarlett, in that really casual way that just makes it obvious how much he's crushing on her. He goes bright red whenever Plum says her name. Plum's really funny, she calls it "going Scarlett," which makes him worse, of course. Plum says to invite Scarlett to my next party so Simon can get off with her. I don't want people at St. Tabby's thinking I ask just anyone to my parties, or they'll all pester me for invitations, but Simon is so rich it's not true. And as Plum says, Scarlett might actually be okay-looking if she bothered to do anything about her appearance.

Eavesdroppers never hear any good of themselves, right? "Might actually be okay-looking." Wow. I feel so flattered.

Actually, what I feel is cross all over again at seeing the part about my only being invited as a present for Simon. You were like a gift bag, Taylor had said when I told her the story. (In America, apparently, guests sometimes receive a present for coming to a party. Weird.)

I was Simon's gift bag. Charming.

I grit my teeth and flick forward again. I've gone too far back. It's hard to find the right place . . . the pages are fine and Nadia's writing is small and tight, the black ink running through the thin paper and making it hard to read.

And then I find it. I can feel my eyes widening as I read, as if it's such a huge piece of information, my irises actually need to get bigger to take it in.

It wasn't Scarlett's fault. It couldn't have been. How could she have known Dan was allergic to nuts? We didn't know, and we were his friends!

No, that's not true. I've got to tell the truth here, even if I can't tell it anywhere else. That's what my therapist says, that's why I'm writing this diary. I have to release the pressure somehow, that's what she says, and here's a good place to start.

Plum knew. She must have known.

I didn't realize what I was seeing at the time. I was looking for fags—I can't believe I'd run out so fast, I really need to cut down—and Plum always has some. So I went to look in her bag. I didn't even bother asking her, we're always in and out of each other's bags for all kinds of stuff. And I knew which one it was—the Marc Jacobs in chestnut with the limited-edition buckle.

There weren't any cigarettes in it after all. Weird. Plum must be running through them even faster than me. I just closed up the bag again and went to see who had some Silk Cut Ultras. And the thing I saw inside . . . I did mean to ask her about it, but the party was raging and it went out of my head. I mean, it was odd, but not that interesting.

But later, when the police were talking to us, I realized what I'd seen in Plum's bag. It was bright yellow—it looked like a big marker pen, and it was in a plastic case with a yellow top. At the time I just thought, what does Plum need a marker pen for? And then I realized, because the police were describing it to us, and asking if we'd seen it.

It was Dan's EpiPen. If he'd had it on him, he wouldn't have died. And it was in Plum's bag.

I can't believe what I'm reading.

I should have asked her about it straightaway. Dan's death was an accident, it must have been! And there's probably some very good explanation for why his EpiPen was in Plum's bag.

And Plum probably didn't tell anyone because it was too late anyway and she was embarrassed.

But it's never good to make Plum feel embarrassed. If I do ask her about it, she'll be so angry with me when I tell her what I saw that she'll send me to Coventry forever and then no one else will talk to me either.

I keep reading, to see if anything else is going to come up. But no. It goes into the bit I've already read, about me coming back to school to pick my stuff up . . . lots of entries about parties, boys, endless whines about how fat she is, details of how far she's run on the treadmill and how little she's eaten that day . . . blah blah blah . . . then the bit about writing the note for me . . . Nothing more about me that I haven't seen already.

I jump up and leave her room, carrying the diary. I remember seeing a lavishly equipped home office off the living room.

Twenty-four

VERY CLEVER INDEED

As I come out of the office, the autumn sunlight is pouring through the French doors, flooding the living room with a warm golden glaze, striking sparks off the glass and chrome of the bar, glinting on the bottles. I know I shouldn't, but I can't help it. I take the diary back to Nadia's room and slip it back exactly where it was on the bookshelf. Then I come back into the living room again, walk over to the bar and sit down on one of the chrome and leather stools, in the same place I was when Dan appeared so magically behind the bar and started chatting me up.

I turn my head and look out onto the terrace. The floor lights are so well concealed that by day I can hardly see where they are. The fountain isn't switched on, but it still looks striking, the wide granite ribbon like modern sculpture. And there's the bench that Dan and I sat on, and there's the stretch of stone path that I went up and down in a handstand, showing off shamelessly to get him to like me.

I gulp, and turn back again. I catch my reflection in the

mirrored glass behind the bar. God, I look scruffy today. I remember what an effort I made that night, my hair, my makeup, tugging at that green silky top to get it to hang just right. I remember checking out the people I could see in the mirror and being awed by how shiny and cool they looked. Those girls sitting down the bar from me in their incredibly sexy backless dresses—I couldn't believe it when Dan actually left them to come back to talk to me again.

It's all as vivid as if it were happening right now. I have a rush of memory, clear and specific in every detail. Dan, turning away from those girls, coming back down the bar toward me, smiling. Me, pushing away those nasty greasy crisps, embarrassed that I'd been eating, when none of the super-slim girls at the party were even going near something that fattening.

Oh my God. The crisps.

I never even thought to mention them to the police, or at the inquest. Everyone asked me what I'd had at the party, what I'd eaten that day, in case I'd had anything that could linger on my mouth and poison Dan. And though I dutifully recited what I'd had for breakfast, lunch, and dinner (all allergen-free, which was what they were concerned about) plus the glass or two of champagne at the party, I forgot all about that handful of crisps until this moment.

Those crisps. They were much oilier than any crisps I've ever eaten before or since. Weirdly oily, now I come to think about it. They left my fingers really greasy.

I'm off the stool in a second. I shoot round the bar and

start dragging every cupboard door open one by one, search-ing through them, a wild idea racing through my head as I remember a cookery program I saw a few months ago on daytime TV, whose bubbly, brightly lipsticked presenter was talking about the best oil to fry chips in.

There's so much stuff in the cupboards that it's over-whelming: lemon squeezers, cocktail shakers, unopened jars of olives and maraschino cherries, cocktail recipe books, boxes of drink stirrers, packets of designer paper napkins with the mind-boggling price still on, spare bottles of mixers and syrups—who *are* these people? Are Nadia's parents rav-ing alcoholics, or do they simply have so much money they don't know what to do with it, and just keep buying useless stuff?

And then, in the third cupboard, I find it. Pushed to the back. You'd never notice it, half hidden as it is behind the shiny blue and green bottles of Curaçao and chartreuse and peppermint liqueur. And even if you did, you'd just pull it out and wonder why on earth someone had put peanut oil in the bar cupboard when really it belonged in the kitchen.

No one but me would know. No one but me would real-ize that someone opened up this bottle of peanut oil and poured just enough of it over a bowlful of crisps for them to soak it up without leaving a telltale pool of oil at the bottom of the bowl. No one but me would realize that that person must have put the bowl on the bar in front of Dan, hoping he'd take some crisps from it. And how happy they must have been when it was me, instead, who ate the crisps, and then kissed Dan with a mouth so saturated in peanut oil that he dropped dead in under two minutes.

How convenient for them! How excited they must have been when I provided the perfect distraction, and completely blurred the link between Dan and what killed him! Everyone—the newspapers, the coroner, even the police— were so swept up in the drama of the situation, me and Dan kissing on the terrace almost as soon as we met, that they can't have bothered to check out the food at the party. I know they asked if there had been any peanuts or any other type of food Dan was allergic to there, and Nadia said no. But they didn't go into it any deeper than that. Because if they had, they would have found the crisps.

Or would they? I wonder. It would have been very easy to get rid of the telltale crisps. You could just chuck them away—you could even eat them, if you weren't allergic to peanut oil yourself. I imagine the person at the party who killed Dan, watching the paramedics rush in, the terrible scene on the terrace, quietly removing that bowl and disposing of it, or even eating the evidence in plain view of everyone, and it makes me shiver right down to the base of my spine.

Dan was murdered. Now I know that for sure.

I push the peanut oil bottle to the very back of the cupboard and pile up everything in front of it. I can't take it to the police yet. It's not enough evidence. By itself, it doesn't prove anything. Also, I'm in here illegally, and I don't need any more trouble with the police, not until I can go to them with the whole story of how Dan was killed laid out for them in black and white. Besides, it's really unlikely to have any fingerprints on it. Wouldn't whoever had dosed the crisps have wiped the bottle down afterward? And then they shoved it in a cupboard with spare stuff that no one probably goes into for years at a time. Much safer than trying to smuggle a liter-big, open bottle of oil out of the house. Very clever of them.

This murderer is very clever indeed.

And just as I think that, I hear a noise that chills my blood. A key in the front door.

At least I manage not to dive back into Nadia's room, though that's my first impulse. I stare around me wildly and then make a dash down the hall—toward the front door, which isn't good, but I know I mustn't be trapped in the back of the apartment, I need to get closer to the exit, and I remember there being a cleaning-supply cupboard next to the kitchen—no one ever goes in the cleaning-supply cupboard, do they? I shoot in there, tripping over a bucket and mop, and I've only just caught my balance and closed the door behind me when I hear the beeping of an alarm at the front door, and then several sharp higher beeps as whoever has just come in taps in the security code on the alarm panel. All the beeping stops.

I ease the door open just a fraction to see who it is. I'm assuming it's Nadia, back early from whatever she was doing with Plum.

Oh God. It's not Nadia.

I said that no one in this house would ever go near the cleaning-supplies cupboard. I forgot about the maid.

●   ●   ●

I know it's the maid because she looks tired and because she's dressed in cheap, brightly colored clothes—a long woolly jumper with a pattern knitted into it, stonewashed jeans, that kind of boot that looks like it's crumpled down over the ankles but is supposed to be like that, for reasons I never understand. I only got a very brief look at her through the crack in the door, but it was instantly obvious that she was wearing clothes that neither Nadia or Nadia's mum would ever dream of putting on. I've often noticed that the chic-er people are, the less color they wear. Some of the St. Tabby's inner circle didn't look as if they owned any items of clothing brighter than beige.

God, why is my brain going on about clothes? I'm trapped in this cupboard with the cleaning lady just down the corridor, and coming closer every moment. I can hear her footsteps on the marble floor! Frantically, I look around for someplace to hide. But it's just shelves, stocked with bleaches and cream cleansers as far as my eye can see. Maybe if I were as thin as Nadia I could hide behind the mop, but with my figure that's definitely not going to work. Oh God, she's going to see me the instant she walks into the room.

The door swings open. There's a deep sigh. I assume that this is because the poor cleaning lady is having to come in and work on Sunday. For a moment she just stands there. Then I hear a heavy rustle and a dull clinking. Pause. Then another, even deeper sigh, and eventually a clank and rattle, like plastic and glass being dropped into something, and then something else sounds like it's being dragged over the tiled floor, and then there are footsteps on the tiles, mercifully directed toward the door, and then the door being pulled to, and she's moving away down the corridor . . .

Very slowly, I let my breath out, bit by bit. I've crammed myself as tight as I could behind the door, but all she'd have had to do was push on it just that bit more and she'd have realized there was something big and squashy in the way, and come round to see what it was, and probably have screamed the place down. I might have been holding my breath, but my heart was pounding so loudly I'm amazed she didn't hear that! Whew. I'm safe for now, but I have to get out of here before she comes back in for something else. She's taken the bucket and mop, so at least I won't fall over those on my way out. Her jacket's hanging up on a peg. I can't believe they don't let her hang her coat up in the hall with everyone else's, but make her hide it away in here. That's so rude.

I give it five minutes and then peer gingerly out of the closet door, easing it open inch by inch. I don't see or hear her, which is good. Gradually, I exit the cupboard, on tenterhooks in case a noise comes and I have to nip back inside again. But what's weird is that I actually don't hear anything at all. This flat is so big that two people can be in it together and not even sense each other's presence.

Still no noise . . . still silence . . . I'm tiptoeing down the corridor, toward the front door, moving faster and faster—I'm at the door now, turning the big deadbolt lock, pulling the door open, nipping through it, and closing it behind me as softly as I can. Still, there's a really loud click as the lock snaps back into place, which completely panics me. I race across the lobby to the lift, pressing the Call button desperately, watching the display as the lift seems to take forever to reach the penthouse floor.

And then, of course, as the doors begin to open I nearly freak, thinking that maybe Nadia has rushed back and is going to be on the other side of them.

But she isn't. I breathe a huge sigh of relief. There's no one in the lift but me reflected in the mirror on the back wall, my expression so panicked that it almost makes me laugh. And I step in, pulling up the hood of my jacket to conceal my face, and hit the Ground Floor button with so much relief that my hand is trembling and fumbles so much I end up stabbing my finger repeatedly at the button, just to make sure.

I walk across the lobby with my hood still up. I thought I was going to have to climb back into the dog kennel lift and find the service entrance to sneak out of. I wasn't bargaining for having to go past the doorman. But I don't have a choice now. And honestly, I'm incredibly grateful. The thought of squashing myself back into that lift, or getting stuck between floors again, was a constant terror in the back of my mind the whole time I was in Penthouse C. Never again am I doing something that stupid. Never again.

The doorman says something to me but I don't turn my head, I just keep walking. He says it louder, but I walk faster. Out of the corner of my eye, I see him coming out from behind the desk, but then the glass doors are sliding open, and I'm walking through them swiftly, breathing fresh air, and nothing's ever felt as good before in my life. I pick up my stride and I'm down the street, losing myself in the crowds of Sunday shoppers, before he can get anywhere near me. I know he can't leave his desk for long, so he'll have turned around by now and gone back in. And even if there's CCTV in the lobby, I had my hood up, so no one could recognize me.

I'm free.

Shoved into my jacket pocket are the photocopies of Nadia's diary that I made in the office. I have evidence now, of a sort. Too early to take to the police, just like the peanut oil bottle in the back of the bar cupboard, but evidence all the same.

I know a lot I didn't know before today.

I know Dan was murdered. I know how he was murdered. And I know that Plum had a part in it, because his EpiPen was in her handbag, and there's absolutely no non-suspicious explanation for that. Was it Plum who poured the peanut oil over the crisps? But why would she do that? This must have been planned in advance. No one could have set this up, right down to the oil stored under the bar, on the spur of the moment.

I'm going to have to do a really thorough investigation of Plum.

I look at my watch. God, I've been in Nadia's place for hours! I'll need to hurry to make it back to school by the dinner bell. The Sunday trains take forever. I squint across at our rendezvous point. Taylor's already gone, as we agreed she should do if I was running late. I start sprinting down the street, heading for the tube station, dashing through the crowds, ducking and weaving past dawdling shoppers without ever slowing down. I can't wait to show Taylor the photocopied pages of Nadia's diary. I know that when she hears what I've found out, that Dan was murdered, it will only make her keener to plan out the next stage of our mystery-solving, to take on a job that she might get one day for real as a grown-up, licensed private detective.

I have a double quest now, and I'm more than ready for the challenge. I'm going to find out who killed Dan. And I'm going to take my revenge on Plum Saybourne. How dare she keep accusing me of being Dan's killer, when all along the EpiPen that would have saved his life was hidden in her handbag! I'm so angry with her that whenever I think about that my hands curl into fists. I'm already plotting ways to have my revenge.

And something tells me that Taylor will be really good at helping with that, too. . . .

Twenty-five

ENOUGH WITH WISHES

I'm racing up the drive. God, that Sunday train was even slower than I was expecting! I paced up and down the carriage as if I had live electricity under my feet, hissing with impatience every time the train jerked to a halt between stations and left me staring at the blank wall of a railway embankment. I'm in a panic that I'll miss the dinner bell, and I'm so keen to tell Taylor everything I've found out that I've run all the way from the station, tearing up the path from Wakefield village. The gravel on the drive is catching in the soles of my sneakers, slowing me down, and I swerve onto the grass instead so that I can pick up full speed again.

Evening sunlight's flooding down through the oak branches and dappling onto the grass. It's so strong that when I catch a flash of red moving through the trees, it takes me a moment to realize what it is.

Jase Barnes. He's dressed up as if he's going out—a

poppy-red shirt that looks great against his dark gold skin, and black jeans that make his long legs look even longer. Wow. He's walking away from me, round the corner of the new school wing, and as I watch, he disappears from view.

My legs are pumping the grass like I'm a sprinter leading the pack, going for the finishing line. I skid off the grass, onto the concrete paving, and execute a perfect ninety-degree turn—not right for the dining hall, but left, heading straight for Jase. I swing round the corner of the building and see him turning down the path that leads to the Barneses' cottage. As soon as my feet start pounding hard concrete, he hears someone running toward him, and swings around. His eyes widen with surprise.

"Scarlett! Where are you *going?*" he exclaims.

I'm all sweaty from running. No makeup, no lip gloss, no high heels, no miniskirt, just a nasty old hoodie and jeans. I'm a foot shorter than him in my trainers. But I don't care about my nonexistent grooming or my midget height or my shiny face. I'm so high on my recent successful spying mission that I feel like I own the world, and the part of it I'm most interested in is standing slap bang in front of me.

I want to plant a flag in this territory, claim it as mine. And before I can think about what the hell I'm doing (because if I do think about it, I'll never get up the nerve to go for it), I jump up on tiptoes and place my hands on his shoulders so I'm barely high enough to reach his lips. And then I kiss him full on the mouth, just long enough to feel my body pressed up against his, the heft of his shoulder muscles under my palms, the hard curves of his chest against mine, the light tangy enticing smell of his aftershave . . .

Oh God, my head is spinning. I swivel on my toes and spin around and shoot off as if the hounds of hell were after me. Which they will be, in the person of Miss Newman, if I don't make it to the dining hall in time. The bell's ringing just as I get there, and as I fall in with the last stragglers pushing to make it through the swing doors on the dot of seven, I look back, gasping for breath. He's still standing there, gaping after me. He raises one hand and feebly flickers his fingers at me: he looks like he's in shock.

There's a grin on my face that feels like it's lighting up the whole of my body. I'm so happy I could literally jump for joy. I turn and dash through the doors, and across the room I see Taylor waving at me madly from the end of a table, her expression one big question mark.

My hand goes up to pat the papers in the inside pocket of my jacket. Still there. I stand for a moment, catching my breath, and then I head across the crowded dining hall in Taylor's direction.

I started out this year with two wishes. Well, enough with wishes. I'm too old for them now. Wishes are just weedy things. I'm making resolutions now.

Number one: solve the mystery of Dan's murder. And number two: get Jase Barnes to be the one who grabs me and kisses me next time. I want him to run up to me, wrap those

259

gorgeous muscular arms of his around me, and kiss me like he'd been thinking about nothing else but doing precisely that since I planted one on him and ran away.

I'd say that was more than enough to be getting on with, wouldn't you?

ABOUT THE AUTHOR

Lauren Henderson was norn in London and lived in Tuscany and Manhattan before returning to London to settle down with one husband and two very fat cats. She has written seven books in the Sam Jones mystery series, which has been optioned for American TV; many short stories; and three romantic comedies. Her nonfiction dating guide, *Jane Austen's Guide to Dating,* has been optioned as a feature film by the writer behind *Ten Things I Hate About You* and *Ella Enchanted.* Lauren's books have been translated into more than twenty languages. With Stella Duffy, she has edited an anthology of women-behaving-badly crime stories, *Tart Noir;* their joint Web site is www.tartcity.com. Lauren has been described as both the Dorothy Parker and the Betty Boop of the crime novel. Her interests include trapeze classes, gymnastics, and eating complex carbohydrates.